The Eagle

Under His Wings Trilogy
Book 3

by

Ronna Bacon

Dedication

To my Heavenly Father, who has provided the words I write. He really does give strength to rise and face each and every day.

Isaiah 40:31 They that wait upon the Lord shall renew their strength. They shall mount up with wings like eagles. They shall walk and not faint. They shall run and not be weary. (KJV)

Table of Contents

Prologue

The sun was high, brilliant and strong, reflecting back from the river's water. He disliked having to mingle like a commoner, wearing clothes off the rack. He shuddered at how long he had to have them on. He wanted his designer clothes back.

His contact was to have left the information he needed on a flash drive for him and was to meet him here. He had to be somewhere in this mess of rocks along the river. He looked down at his hands and wished he had gloves he could put on.

Only thing - it looked different from the picture he was sent. Something had changed. Something had been moved. Anger rose within him. That fool. He must have sent the wrong picture.

He pulled out his phone and brought up the text with the picture and looked. He was in the right area but the man isn't there. If he wasn't there, that meant his package wouldn't be either, unless he had dropped it and was afraid to tell him.

He would have to come back later when there were fewer people and search again. Once he had that information, then he would be set.

Chapter 1

Liam Bradley stood on the banks of the river and watched the water flowing by. The sun was low in the sky and it was cooling off a bit from the heat of the day. This was a favourite time of day, work was done, he could relax. He raised his eyes and studied the rock formation along the river. He found them an inspiration for his work as a landscaper. Many times, he had worked in some form of his inspiration from here. He had a new contract, a family just moved to the area in the last six months, who wanted a rugged look to their yard and a waterfall. They had had outbuildings erected that he would be working around, but he was up to it.

He moved his line of sight and watched a black and white dog at play in the shallow area. He searched the tree line and spotted its owner, standing back.

The form moved forward and Liam saw it was a female but she was too far away for him to identify her. He looked back at the dog. It wasn't one he was familiar with. Tourist season brought a lot of people to the area and many brought their animals as well.

He watched the woman and her dog play, then turned and made his way further along the river bank, to a more rugged area. He needed to watch, it was sometimes slippery if the wind had been blowing the spray from the small area of rapids.

He turned once again and looked behind him and down the river. He never grew tired of watching the water. He turned with his back to the river and ran his eyes along the rocks and bushes. This was what he was trying to envision for the new site. A glint of light caught his eye and he reached forward. Picking up a small plastic container, he turned it over, studying it, and then tucked it into his pocket.

A movement to his right startled him. A sudden yell and he was falling. He felt the water cover him and then his head hit rock. His vision faded. He didn't feel himself tumbling down the river or rising to the surface.

Ashling Downie heard the shout and looked around. Teagan, her Sheltie, stopped, barked and then dove into the water, headed for the other shore. Ashling raced for the water, stopped and then heart in mouth, dove in as well, swimming for the body she saw. She reached it and pulled it up on the riverbank she had just left. It was closest. She felt for a heart beat. He was alive but unconscious. Reaching for the phone she had dropped, she called for help and then waited.

She studied the man's face and frowned. She thought she knew him, had seen him around, but she couldn't place him. Teagan crowded close at the man's side and laid her head on his arm. She then watched Ashling, intelligent brown eyes never wavering.

A sound behind her and she spun. Paramedics were coming towards her, with police officers right behind them. She stood and called Teagan away. Moving further back, she stood and watched as they worked on the unconscious victim and then carried him away.

She breathed a prayer that he would be all right and then turned to walk away. An older gentleman stood near her. Ben Johnson, she knew him from church and as a senior police officer. She sighed, guessed she wouldn't be going anywhere anytime soon to get into dry clothes, and prepared herself to talk to him.

Ben studied the young woman in front of him. He knew she wasn't happy about having to stay but he needed her statement.

"Ashling Downie," Ben spoke. "What happened?"

Ashling looked back at the water, then at Ben, and shrugged. "I really don't know. Teagan and I were playing here at the water. I was doing some training with her. She just alerted and dove into the water. I saw what she was after and went in too." She shrugged. "Isn't that what anyone would do?"

Ben shook his head. "Not always." He looked around. "This is one of Liam's favourite areas of the river. He spends a lot of time here."

"If that's all, I need to go. It's starting to get cold."

Ben looked at her, then down to her dog. "Come on. I'll give you a lift."

As they turned to walk away, Ashling hesitated. She felt eyes on her but could see no one. What was that about?

Caleb Logan, police chief for Riverville, brought his vehicle to a stop near the emergency entrance of the hospital. He hesitated before he got out and said a prayer for his friend. Ben had called him, letting him know that Liam was on his way in by ambulance. He shook his head as he got out. What next for this family: Laycee and his own brother, Joshua, last year, Leith and his now fiancee, six months ago, all targeted for murder and that by upstanding members, or so he thought, of their community.

He stepped inside and looked around, then headed for his brother and his wife. They were newlyweds, just wed about six weeks. Joshua saw him and stood, coming towards him.

"How is he?" Caleb asked.

"They're still working on him. They haven't said much."

Caleb tilted his head to look at Laycee, her long black hair hiding her face. "How's Laycee?"

His brother shrugged. "She's not saying much. I sort of expected that though. She's very vocal with Liam, but with something like this, she can get very quiet."

"Where's Leith and Regan?"

"They were still on a job site and had to finish what they had going. They'll be here as soon as they can."

Caleb laid his hand on his brother's shoulder and then headed back into the exam room area. He wanted answers and he didn't want to wait for them. Something had happened and he wanted to know what. Liam was not one who was careless and lost his footing that easily. He had a bad feeling that once again he would be searching for answers while trying to protect a friend.

He spotted Dr. Young coming from a room and spoke with him, then stepped into the exam room where Liam was lying wrapped in heated blankets, with an IV dripping into his veins. Liam's eyes were closed, his face pale and wan. He had blood on the left side of his head, likely from the fall onto the rocks, Caleb surmised. He stood for a few minutes watching and then turned. Dr. Young had said it would be a while and he had things to do. He would be back, but first he needed to catch up with Ben.

Ashling hesitated at the waiting room door. She had come to see how Liam was but didn't know the family well enough just to walk up to them. If Leith's Regan was here, she would feel more comfortable. She moved to the side to let newcomers move around, then heard someone say her name.

She turned to see Regan Evans beside her.

"Hi, Regan. I just wanted to see how Liam is."

Regan studied her for a moment, then reached out to touch her still damp hair. "You're the one. Eddie said a woman had pulled Liam out. It was you." She reached to hug Ashling, then keeping an arm around her, drew her along with her to the others.

Laycee and Leith turned as Regan approached, eying the newcomer.

"Laycee, Leith, you have met Ashling Downie before. She's the one who pulled Liam out."

Laycee's mouth went into an "O", then she was hugging Ashling. Tears were on her face and she couldn't speak. Ashling's eyes met Leith tear-filled ones. She smiled and nodded at his thank you.

Dr. Young appeared beside them and spoke.

"He's had quite a blow to the head and has the headache to match. No concussion. Lungs are fine. I would like to keep him here for a while just to make sure, but he can go home later. Which one of you will be the one who has to watch him?"

Leith spoke up. "I am."

"He should be good to go in about two hours. I'll have the nurse find you."

Laycee turned to watch him walk away. Joshua studied his wife's face.

"What's bugging you, Laycee?"

She shook her head. "I don't know. There's just something different about Dr. Young. I can't put my finger on it. He's changed."

As the rest studied Laycee's face, Ashling stepped back. She had found out what she wanted and now she was going to head home and let them be by themselves. She smiled in greeting as Pastor Paul, their minister, went by her. Good, she thought. That is what they need.

She was crossing the pavement to her car when she once again heard her name. She turned, and Leith stood behind her.

She held up her hand. "No, Leith, don't say it. No more thanks. No more comments. I was there and so was Teagan. She's the one who really deserves the thanks. If she hadn't seen him, I wouldn't have."

Leith stood, hands deep in the front pockets of his jeans. He looked to the night sky and then back to the woman front of him, half in the shadows. "I do mean thank you." He held up his hand as she protested. "No, you don't understand. He's my only brother. He's the one who has held our family together for so many years since we lost our parents. He's the one who watches and protects us. Without him, our family wouldn't be the same. It would be damaged in a way that I don't want to even imagine." He paused. "What I was going to ask. I know you do dog training. With things the way they are now, I would like to have better training for my Abby and also for Laycee's Defiant. Let me know what we can work out." He stopped, started to say something else, and then turned and walked back to the hospital.

Ashling's hand came to her mouth and she hesitated, almost going after him, then turned to her car. She would come up with a plan. She didn't know all the history yet but she would find out what they were so afraid of.

****

He watched from the shadows near the door. He had to find out if they knew anything. He had to find that flash drive. He wanted out of this town. That was the only way he knew how. His occupation didn't let him save what he wanted to save. If they had it, they would pay. He turned and walked back to his tasks. One day, one day very soon, he hoped.

Chapter 2

Liam moved his head. It hurt. He opened his eyes. That hurt. He could hear someone near him, but it seemed just too much of an effort to wake up.

A hand on his shoulder roused him again. "Liam, come on, buddy. Time to wake up."

Liam squinted at the voice and groaned, "Go away, Leith. This isn't funny."

He heard a small laugh, then Leith spoke again, "No, it's not, Liam, but we need to get you up. You've been discharged and they need your bed for someone who is really sick."

Liam's eyes opened wider and he looked around. He was in a hospital room. How did he get here?

His eyes closed as Leith raised the head of his bed. As things steadied, he reopened them. He stared at his brother, headache pounding behind his eyes.

"Dr. Young has discharged you. You have a choice—my place or Laycee's."

Liam glared at his brother, then sighed. "Yours. Tell me what happened. I don't remember."

Leith perched on the side of the bed, and watched his brother. "You were fished out of the river. Somehow you fell in and hit your head. If Ashling and her dog hadn't been there, you wouldn't be here."

Liam puzzled at this, then shook his head, regretting it instantly. "I don't even remember being near the river."

Leith stood. "It may or may not come back to you. Come on. Let's get you home."

Moving slowly, Liam managed to dress and then make his way to his brother's truck.

"Where's Laycee?"

"Likely waiting for you at my place."

"Great. I don't need that."

"Whether you need it or not, accept it. It's our turn to give back to you."

Liam turned his head to look at Leith. Leith's eyes were straight ahead, not looking at him. "I'm sorry, Leith. I'm grumpy and have a rotten headache. That was uncalled for."

Leith slanted him a look and then a smile. "You have always been one to give, not accept. It's your turn to accept." Leith stopped, then spoke, "God was with you today, Liam. I don't know if I could have handled losing you."

Liam was silent. He didn't feel he could respond. Leith was right. God had protected him. He sighed to himself. Now he just had to get rid of the headache so he could go to work tomorrow, and he already knew Laycee would be on his case.

Liam headed into his office in the morning. He wasn't up to working at any of the job sites his landscaping business had going. Maybe in the afternoon his head would be well enough that he could.

His foreman, Bud Whalen, was waiting for him. Liam went over the work they had on the go, then sent Bud out to the sites.

He sat back in his desk chair. His head was aching, but not like last night. He just couldn't remember what had happened. He tried to work for a while, then in frustration, threw down his pencil, got up and walked out of the office. He kept walking, heading to the river. He needed to see for himself where it happened. He didn't remember being there at all.

Liam stood, watching the peaceful flow of the water. Last night, it had almost taken his life. Today, it was serene. He looked up at the sky. "God, You were there last night. You saved me. Thank you."

When he looked back down, he shuddered at how close it had been last night. He turned to study the ground where he was standing, then walked further along the river bank. How had he slipped? He knew this area so well and was cautious walking it.

Footsteps sounded behind him and he spun. Eddie Brown, a town police officer but also a good friend, stood there, watching him.

"Liam. Good to see you upright and out and about."

Liam reached to shake his hand. "I hear I had quite the adventure."

"That you did. If it hadn't been for that dog, no one would have found you until it was too late." Eddie looked at him and then around. "What I don't understand, Liam, is this. How did you slip? You're way too cautious."

Liam nodded. "That's what I'm trying to figure out." He searched the area, then stopped. "I was about here. Eddie, I wasn't on the rocks that were wet. I was over by this one." He paced over to a larger rock. "I just can't remember why."

Eddie came to stand beside him, studying where Liam had been standing, then turning to look at the riverbank and the river. He paced to the edge of the river and back.

Liam stood silent, watching him, his mind racing at the possibilities.

Eddie sighed. "It's what we were afraid of, Liam. It wasn't an accident."

Liam's eyes shot to Eddie's and then slid shut. "Who?"

Eddie shook his head. "That's what we now have to figure out. Come on, Liam. Let's get out of here." He turned to leave, then stopped. "It's the unknown, not knowing who, that is going to be the problem. You three Bradleys - you're well liked in the community. Your parents were. Your family goes back to the founding of the town. But please, Laycee and Leith's adventures in the last few months have been enough. We don't need you going on an adventure like that."

Liam stared at him. "You don't think…" His voice trailed away and then he walked past Ben. "As far as I know, I have no enemies. I was just in the wrong place at the wrong time."

Eddie's voice drifted after him. "But who decided you were in the wrong place at the wrong time?"

Ashling headed towards the local cafe. She had discovered it shortly after the family have moved to town. It was Friday, and she knew SueEllen always had freshly made scones on the menu. She planned to pick up some and take back to her parents' pet store for their morning tea.

A voice calling her name stopped her and she turned. It was Laycee Logan.

"Wait up a minute, Ashling." Laycee hurried to catch up. "I can't keep up with you. You're too fast."

Ashling grinned. "That's what I'm told. Always in a rush. It's the running I do. You need to come with me some morning."

Laycee tilted her head and thought. "I certainly do. Now if I could just find the time. What I wanted to ask. Would you be willing to come speak to our therapy group some time? Your choice of topic."

Ashling looked around, then said, "I don't like public speaking. I'm not comfortable in that. One on one is fine. I would really have to pray about that."

Laycee nodded. "Do and then let me know. I don't want to pressure you." She looked past her. "There're Leith and Liam. I need to catch up with them. Please call me." Laycee started away, then turned back. "I would really like to have you as a friend. Let me know when we can get together for coffee or a meal."

A surprised look came across Ashling's face. "As long as it's tea and not coffee, you're on."

As Laycee caught up with her brothers, they looked up. Leith's hand came up in a wave to Ashling. She could feel Liam studying her, puzzling out who she was. Ashling shrugged, then continued on her way. She really wanted those scones for their morning break.

The three Bradly siblings settled into their booth in the cafe and gave their orders. Liam studied his brother and sister. God had spared their lives through kidnappings and murders in the last few month, Laycee because of an accountant involved in financial fraud, Leith because of a jeweller smuggling stolen uncut gems. He listened to their chatter and his mind drifted off to the plans he should be working on.

A hand on his arm brought him out of his reverie. Laycee was watching him.

"You didn't hear what we said," she accused. "You're off in that world of planning again aren't you?"

He nodded. "I guess I was. So what had you asked?"

"Leith and Regan have an idea about their wedding and they want our input. Can you stay with us for a while or should we let the senior toddle off back to his office?"

Liam laughed, caught his sister in a hug, and dropped a kiss on her black curls. "I'm listening, I'm listening." He caught Leith's eyes and stopped. There was a seriousness there that seldom showed, not that deep. He would have to question him with Laycee wasn't around.

Laycee finally stood. "I need to get going. I'll see you all later."

They watched their sister walk away, then Liam turned to Leith. "Ok, give. What are you thinking about?"

Leith studied his almost empty coffee cup. He was finding it hard to put into words what he wanted to say. He knew he wouldn't be able to if he looked at Liam. "It's...It's..."His voice kept dying away.

Liam's voice was laced with amusement as he spoke. "That's not like you. You're never at a loss for words."

Leith tossed a balled up napkin at his brother. "We could have lost you last night, Liam. I'm not ready for that. And I don't think it was an accident." He stopped, looked up, and then at his brother. Liam was shaken at the depths of emotion Leith showed, something he so seldom did. "I think you're being targeted too, just like Laycee and I were. If God had not protected you, you would have died."

Liam leaned forward, arms on the table. "I doubt it. I think I was just a bit clumsy and slipped."

Leith stood. "Think what you will. I don't think that way. Change of subject, come on. I need to get some food for the critters and you need to come help me."

Liam protested. "They're your animals, yours and Regan. Why do I have to help?"

****

The Colonel sat in his office, rage building within him. He needed that flash drive. If only the fool who had it had been smarter. Planning a drop by the river—that was a childish game. Now he was facing ruin. He needed that information, then he could leave this town.

He picked up his phone, made a call, and set in play a plan that would not be stopped. He rested his hand for a minute on the phone, then picked up his pen and began his paperwork. His rage burned but just maybe now he would be safe.

Chapter 3

Leith swung open the door to the Downie's Fur and Feathers pet store, then stepped back to let a customer out. Liam followed him through the door and then stood looking around. He didn't have pets, had no occasion to shop in a pet store, but this place was clean and tidy. He could vaguely remember when it hadn't been under the previous owners.

At the sound of a female voice, his attention to turned to the counter. A young woman was finishing up an order for a customer who he realized was Dr. Young's wife. When she turned to leave, she looked discontented and unhappy.

"We'll have that delivered this afternoon for you, Mrs. Young. Either Lorcan or I will bring it by."

A voice could be heard, "Good bye. Good bye. Don't come back." Mrs. Young stopped, then Liam saw the disgust and anger in her face. What was going on?

Leith raised a hand on the way by the counter.

"Morning, Leith. The food you wanted for Abby is on the shelf and Emmy's food is as well."

"Thanks, Ashling."

The woman had not looked up from the paperwork she had moved to. Liam watched in fascination as a small green bird hopped down the counter and then up on her shoulder.

"Sally good."

"No, Sally's not good. Sally's a bad bird."

"Sally good bird. Sally pretty bird."

"Sally is a pretty bad bird."

Sally slid along the shoulder and tucked her head close to the woman's face. "Sally good. Sally good."

"No Sally, you're not. You weren't nice to the customer."

"Sally nice."

"Sally, you need to behave. Next time she comes in, you're in your cage."

"Sally good. No cage."

Startling blue eyes raised for a moment and caught Liam's, then dropped. By this time, Leith had set the bags of food on the counter and was grinning. A young man had entered behind the counter, also grinning. Leith assumed it was the woman's brother, their features were so alike.

"Sally, don't argue. You know you were bad. Now to your cage."

"Sally pretty. Sally good. No cage." The bird then let out a chorus of notes.

"Ashling, you know you can't win with her."

"Shut up, Lorcan. It's your fault. You just had to teach a macaw to talk, didn't you?"

By this time, Leith's head was buried in his arms on the counter, body shaking with laughter. Lorcan let out a shout of laughter. This startled Sally, who fluffed her feathers, hopped back to the counter, and looked around. She then spied Liam and headed for him.

"Sally, no. You're not a good girl today. Bad girls go to the cage." Ashling reached under the counter and pulled out some pieces of fruit and a few toys. She tapped a toy and said, "Here, Sally. To your cage."

By this time, Sally was on Liam's shoulder, cuddling into his neck. Liam stood still. He had never had a bird on his shoulder before, let alone one who talked. He shot a look at Leith for help, and saw that obviously no help would be coming from that direction.

"Sally, come. Your cage."

"Sally good. Sally stay."

"No, Sally, you're not good. To your cage."

"Sally love. Sally stay."

A stern note came into Ashling's voice. "Enough, Sally. Here's your treat. To your cage." Without looking up from her paperwork, she pointed to the end of the counter where a cage rested. "If you don't you'll not get out again today."

Sally looked at Liam, looked at her treat, then back at Liam. She finally hopped to the counter towards Ashling. Ashling had gathered up her paperwork, clipped it together and set it aside. The whole conversation with the bird had been done while she was working. Liam assumed this was a longstanding debate between the two.

Sally came forward, took her treat and headed for her cage. Once inside, she dropped her treat. "Sally good. Sally pretty."

This sent Leith and Lorcan into fresh gales of laughter.

"Don't encourage her, you two. Next time, you get to deal with her." Ashling came around the counter. "Just for that, Lorcan, you get to stay and watch the store until Da or Mam come."

Liam watched her walk towards him. She tucked her hand under his elbow and turned him back to the door. "We adults are leaving. You children can stay and play with Sally."

The door opened to fresh gales of laughter as they reached it and Caitlin Downie entered. She took a look at the two at the door and then at the two men at the counter.

"Sally again."

"Yes, Mam, Sally again. She's decided she's in love and has been flirting with the customers."

Caitlin laughed. "Then get him out of here before she decides she needs to flirt again."

Ashling steered Liam out of the store and down the street. Letting go of his arm, she turned. "Now that I've rescued you, I should apologize. Sally's a miniature macaw and Lorcan just had to teach her to talk and sing."

Liam stopped her. He stood staring down at her. Brilliant blue eyes and golden blond hair sparkled in the sun. He was over six feet in height but the top of her head easily reached his chin. "No. It's the other way around. You rescued me last night."

Ashling shook her head. "It was really Teagan." At his puzzled look, she continued, "My dog. She saw you and went after you. If she hadn't, I wouldn't have seen you." She looked around, uncomfortable. "I didn't do anything that someone else would not have done."

"Can I at least buy you a cup of coffee?"

Ashling studied him. "No but a cup of tea will do. I don't know how you can swallow that horrid stuff."

Liam laughed, then looked around. "There." He pointed to a street vendor.

"Gail always has a nice selection of teas as well as coffee."

Cradling her cup of tea, Ashling stood and looked at the town around her. It was busy with tourists but she was beginning to recognize a lot of local people. Liam nodded to a park bench that was empty and they headed there.

Liam sat, at a loss for words. This was unusual for him. He watched Ashling as she sat beside him.

"I know you don't think you did much, Ashling. If you hadn't been there." He shuddered at the thought.

She turned to watch his face. "God knew I was needed there. I usually don't go out there at that time of night. I usually have classes." At his look, she continued, "My Teagan and I are competitive, working in agility and herding. I also teach dog classes, obedience, that kind of stuff. Last night, I just had to go. God compelled me to that spot. He knew you would need Teagan."

Liam thought about what she said. Lately, his faith had slipped. Sure he was still in church, still read his Bible, still spent time in prayer, but the spark had faded. He need to re-ignite it but didn't quite know how.

Ashling turned to gaze across the town square. "I'm getting to know your family. Both Laycee and Leith have said you are the eagle in their family. That you have always watched out for them, have protected them. Laycee described you to me as the one who seems tireless, relentless in his search for God." Her eyes turned back to him. "I sense that you are really struggling, that the events of the last months have really tried your faith. God understands when we struggle and doubt. Let Him gather you under His wings and rest for a while, Liam."

Liam stared, astounded that she had read him so well. How was that? He liked the bit of accent he heard peeking through her voice, its cadence sending peace through him. "You have described it well, Ashling. I really do struggle. I haven't said anything to anyone though. How did you know?"

Ashling shrugged. "I just do. Da says it's a gift. Sometimes it feels like a curse. Mam always tells me that intuition should never be ignored but strengthened and followed. It may be the Irish in me, but more likely God." She finished her tea and then stood. "I know you have things you need to get to. My prayers are with you."

Liam watched as she strode away, movements loose and free. She's a runner, he thought. Interesting. I'll have to see if she wants a partner to run with. He then thought about what she said. Yes, she had him pegged. He was struggling. He sighed. I guess I need to speak with Pastor Paul, he thought. A sudden shiver ran through him and he looked around. He could feel eyes on him but couldn't see anyone watching him. Suddenly, he felt very vulnerable in the open, even with people around him.

Dropping his cup in the trash, he headed back for his office.

Caleb looked up as Ben tapped at his door. He motioned him in and Ben dropped into a chair in front of the desk.

"I'm getting too old for all these hours. It's wearing me out, some days."

Caleb waited. He knew Ben really didn't feel like that.

Ben eyed him, then continued, "That new K9 program just might take off. Lorcan Downie's training from the other force is really going to pay off. Once he can find the right partner and get the dog trained, it will really add to our department."

Caleb nodded. "It will. You taking on the training on the evidence side is really helping. Our officers are getting much better, and they were good before." Caleb looked down and then back up. "But that's not why you're here."

Ben shook his head. "No. I've been hearing scuttlebutt from the street and so has Eddie. Liam's fall last night, it wasn't an accident. He was pushed."

Caleb stilled, studying Ben. "That's what we thought. It just didn't look right, or sit right with me."

Ben stood. "Now we just have to figure out who and why. I hope we don't have another Laycee or Leith."

Caleb agreed. "No. That was enough."

Ben didn't know how prophetic his words would turn out to be.

Chapter 4

The Colonel watched as Liam walked away from the town square. He was sure he had something of his. He just needed to find it. The Major had said he had two men that would be able to do that very task. If not, then he would see. He just wanted out of this town. He had had enough.

****

Liam's steps lagged as he approached his home. It had been a long day and he was tired. All he wanted to do was take something for his headache and then lie down. Food didn't interest him.

He reached with his key for the lock and stopped. Something wasn't right. He touched the door and it swung open. Not again, he thought. Not someone going through his stuff. It had been bad enough with the other two, now him?

He stepped away, pulled out his phone, and made the call.

Ben and Eddie approached as he leaned against his truck, watching the activity. Eddie handed him a coffee.

Liam took it with a word of thanks. "Don't say it."

Ben smiled, then sobered. "I was hoping it had been an accident last night, Liam. This makes it seem like it's not."

Liam sighed, took a sip of his coffee, shook his head and then regretted it. Squinting, he looked at the two. "Somehow, I thought you would say that."

Ben studied him. "What is it with you three? First Laycee, then Leith. You just couldn't let them get ahead of you, could you? You really didn't have to join them, you know."

Liam smirked. "I know." He glanced up at the darkening sky. "I just wanted to come home, take something for the headache and go to bed."

Eddie took a look at him, stepped away and then returned, holding out something. "Here's your pain medication. The kitchen has been cleared so it's okay. Now take it."

Ben continued to watch his young friend. He could see past the pain, to how tired he really was. The last year or so had put a lot of strain on him and he was beginning to crack. It was subtle unless you knew him well. Ben really didn't know how well Liam would be able to handle what he feared was coming. His eyes met Eddie and he could see Eddie felt the same. How could they protect him when they had no idea from whom or what? It felt like the last year just wasn't going to end any time soon.

Eddie nodded towards the house and Ben turned. The crime team was finished and they could enter the house.

Liam pushed himself away from the truck, momentarily staggering. Eddie reached to steady him. Liam shrugged his hand away and moved to his home. He hesitated, took a deep breath and entered. There was not much of a disturbance. He had been afraid it would have been worse. He wandered through his house, taking note of where things had been disturbed.

Ben and Eddie watched as he paused at the stairs. Liam took a breath and then slowly climbed them, the two other men on his heels. Liam went through each of the three bedrooms and their attached baths. Ben noted that his house has been upgraded nicely. It had been pretty run down when Liam purchased it. Both Joshua, a renovator, and Leith, a tile setter, had been involved.

Liam stood at his dresser, staring down at the top, not really seeing anything. "I don't see anything missing. That's so strange. I have nothing anyone would want." He turned, brown eyes showing his fatigue.

Ben nodded. "The team didn't find much. Whoever it was, they were thorough but tidy. That's not your usual snatch and grab thief. They also weren't destructive. That tells me they wanted to get in and out without you knowing."

Eddie stepped away to speak with an officer, then stepped back. "It looks as if you just missed them, Liam. We checked your alarm system. The alarm was turned off about 20 minutes before you got home."

Liam paled and then sank down on his bed, eyes closing. "Who? I don't have any enemies. I don't have competition. Not many people want the hard and dirty work I do."

Ben and Eddie exchanged a glance. "Liam, we need to get your locks changed and that's not happening tonight. We are going to post a patrol here for the night, but you shouldn't be here on your own."

As Liam looked up in protest, Ben continued, "We need to keep you safe. You have a choice: spend the night with Laycee or Leith or spend the night at either Eddie's place or mine or even Caleb's. You're too tired and sore to think straight. Let us help you. Don't protest, either."

Liam looked down in shame. That exactly what he had been about to do. "You're right. I'm not thinking straight." He squinted against the pain. "So, who wins the coin toss?"

Eddie smiled. "Come with me. I'm playing bachelor for a few days while my sweetheart's away with her parents."

Later that evening, Caleb tapped at Eddie's door and then followed Eddie through the beautifully decorated bungalow to the kitchen. Eddie made Caleb his tea and then sat down at the table with a mug of coffee.

"How is he?"

"He's sleeping. Wouldn't eat anything. I checked on him about 10 minutes ago. He is worn to the bone right now, I'd say," Eddie replied. "He wasn't happy about not staying at his place. We didn't give him an option. If he had refused, Ben was ready to lock him up."

Caleb laughed softly. "That sounds like Liam. Did the team find anything?"

Eddie shook his head. "Not that I know of. Whoever it was, they were professional. In, search without disturbing much, then out. It just worries me as to how close it came for Liam actually being there."

Caleb nodded. "I know. I just wish I could figure it out."

The men talked quietly for another thirty minutes or so and then Caleb rose to leave.

"We need to have someone stick close to him and he's not going to like it. Who do we have that likes landscaping?"

Eddie thought for a minute. "I hear he's going to being working at the Downie's starting in the next couple of days. I wonder if Lorcan would like to get his hands dirty."

Caleb thought, then smiled. "Perfect. Protection without it being obvious."

****

Things were definitely not going well, the Major thought. His two men hadn't found what he sent them after and had just missed being spotted. The Colonel would not be happy. Right now, the Major wasn't answering his phone. Until he could speak more thoroughly with the men, he wouldn't. These men were professionals. They knew how to find hidden items and had reported that it wasn't in Liam's house. That meant they now needed to search his office and shop. That was going to be a whole lot trickier.

Chapter 5

Liam struggled the next morning. He was more tired and sore than he wanted to admit, but he needed to be on the job. They were headed to the Downie's to start that project. He wanted to be on site for that one as much as he could.

Eddie watched closely as Liam entered the kitchen. He didn't say anything, just handed him a plate of food and a mug of coffee.

"I'll take you to get your truck before heading to the office and check your place out. Ben said Andy would be there early to do your locks and would drop off keys for you at your office." Eddie continued, "I know you feel like we're smothering you, Liam, but something is up and we need to find out what."

Liam sighed. "I know in my head that's why you're doing it. I just can't accept it that I'm a target."

"I know. People who are targets quite often feel that way."

"Thanks, Eddie, for stepping in last night. You and Ben were right. I shouldn't have been on my own."

Eddie smiled and nodded. He knew it was hard for Liam to admit that.

Ashling stood on the back deck and watched the activity in front of her. It was like watching a bunch of ants, she thought, scurrying around, looking as if they didn't have a clue what they were doing, yet accomplishing much. It would be interesting to see Liam's plans come to life.

She turned as the door behind her opened. Her mother came to stand beside her and handed her a cup of tea.

"Thanks, Mam."

"It's going to be a busy few weeks here, my dear. How is that going to affect your classes?"

"Most of them are at night, which will be okay. It's after the men have left for the day. The others, we'll use the work as a distraction test and see how it goes. If we can work in the far building, we should be okay."

"You've thought it through, just as I knew you would. I'm off to the store."

"Don't let Sally flirt with any more customers, Mam."

Caitlin started to laugh. "I would have loved to have seen Liam's face yesterday."

"It was priceless," Ashling agreed, laughing with her Mam. "He really didn't know what to do. And to have that little pest say Sally love must have really floored him. What was Lorcan thinking?"

"You know Lorcan, he finds humour in the most unexpected places."

"That he does."

Liam stood and scanned the area at the end of the day. It was starting to look like just maybe something was going on. It had been a week they had been working here and he was pleased. His body was back to normal and he had been able to put in a good day's work. He turned as he heard Lorcan come up beside him.

"Have you seen where Ashling has her classes?" When Liam shook his head, Lorcan motioned for him to follow. "I thought you had. She's out there now but doesn't have classes tonight. I'll show you."

Liam followed Lorcan to one of the outbuildings. He was surprised when he entered and saw the spacious lay out, the kennels built in along the side, a dog grooming area at one end. Someone had put a lot of thought into the planning.

Ashling turned as she heard them. Liam thought she looked tired. He knew she had been putting in longer hours at the store and also at night.

"Lorcan, did you find out about that lab?"

"I did. Can you spare some time tomorrow or should I pick her up and bring her here?"

Ashling thought. "Either one, though off her home territory may give up a better sense of her personality. See if you can get Suzanne to bring her over sometime tomorrow night. No, that won't work."

Lorcan stared at his sister who stared back. Liam's eyes flew between the two. He knew they were communicating silently but it sure looked like a battle from where he stood. Lorcan's eyes finally dropped.

"You're right. Tomorrow night is booked. I forgot. How about Monday night?"

"That should work. If she can be here around 6."

Lorcan turned to leave, then stopped. He went to say something and then shook his head and left.

Ashling watched him walk away and then turned to Liam. "You've never made it back here. I thought you would have."

Liam gave a gentle smile. "I was never asked. It's your work place. I didn't want to intrude."

Ashling tucked her hand into his arm and led him forward. "Then let's give you a tour. Teagan is around somewhere as well."

Liam had to admit to himself he liked the feel of her hand tucked into his arm. It felt right. Maybe it was time he thought seriously about dating and marriage. He just hadn't before, but now Laycee and Leith were settled. He listened to her soothing voice with just the hint of the Irish accent in her parents' voices describing the training building.

"You've put a lot of thought into this," he said.

"I did. I worked in some great centres and have always had this dream of having my own. It's a lot of work but it's so worth it. I think you understand."

He nodded. "I do." He stopped walking, and turning to her, studied her profile. She had a peaceful look about her, a calmness that flowed and calmed those around her. He started as she began to giggle.

"I'm sorry. I just keep thinking of the look on your face when Sally was on your shoulder."

"You're not sorry." Liam laughed. "She is quite the bird. Did Lorcan really teach her?"

Ashling nodded. "He did. He has such a dry sense of humour at times and teaching Sally just seemed to fit."

"Ashling." Liam hesitated and she turned to look at him. "We haven't know each other a long time." Again he stopped and searched the far end of the building. "Would you be willing to go out for a meal with me?"

Ashling tilted her head to study him, and then turned and walked outside. Liam's heart sank. He had blown it. He followed her. She was standing, arms around her waist.

"I'm sorry. I shouldn't have asked."

Ashling shook her head. "No, it just took me by surprise, that's all. When were you thinking?"

Liam shrugged. "I don't know. I guess I really wasn't."

Ashling started to laugh again and Liam joined in. "Liam, you really should have thought this through, you know?" she teased him. "Okay, so what's your schedule like for the next couple of days? I don't have anything on other than the store and I know Da and Mam will cover. That is except for some specialized training with Teagan, and she could use a day off from that."

Liam thought through his work schedule. Tomorrow would do. He had booked the work time line so that weekends out be free for his men. They put in long hours and he knew having two days off in a row were needed to help refresh them. "How about tomorrow?"

She thought and then nodded. "Okay, just let me know what time."

"How about 11? That way, we can go somewhere for lunch and then maybe a nice walk."

"Oh that's it, is it? First, lunch and then a walk. You drive a hard bargain, Mr. Liam Bradley. I agree."

****

The Major watched from the tree line. He lowered his binoculars and waited. Somehow he was going to have to approach them and find out if they had that information. He wondered if they did now. If they had and the police had it, the Colonel would have been arrested.

He looked behind him at a slight noise and faded back into the trees. He couldn't be seen. He would have to have the Sergeants start following them. That was the only way. If it came to it, then the Sergeants would bring those two to him.   He didn't want to report another mission failure.

Chapter 6

Liam pulled up to the Downie's home and stopped. He was nervous. It had been so many years since he had asked out a woman on a date. He approached the door and knocked. Lorcan, heading out for work in their store, opened the door, looked him over from head to toe, and then grinned.

"She's ready. Go on back to the kitchen." Lorcan stopped as he walked by Liam and came back. "Be patient with her, Liam. She's been hurt in the past and underneath that strong, calm veneer, she is fragile."

Liam took a look at her brother. "No, she's really not, Lorcan. She's a lot stronger than you think."

Lorcan shook his head. Liam had it bad all right.

Liam followed female voices to the kitchen and found Ashling and Caitlin in a hot debate. His eyes bounced between the two woman. Neither was backing down and it seemed as if neither was the winner.

A hand of his shoulder made his turn. Ashling's father, Lachlan, stood beside him, a grin on his face. Liam could see the strong resemblance to Lorcan.

"They're not mad. It's how they discuss things at time. You'll get used to it."

Liam's eyes flew to Lachlan's, who grinned again. "You have it bad for my daughter, I can see, my boy. We'll talk when the time's right." A quick squeeze and Lachlan headed for his wife and daughter.

"Okay, my girls. Time's up. Liam's here and waiting, Ashling. Go, enjoy your day."

Ashling turned, her face flushing as she realized he had been standing there for a while. He grinned at her in amusement. Another facet of her personality was showing.

Caitlin laughed. "Hello, Liam. Welcome to our more common mode of speaking in the morning. It's not all quiet talk and hugs."

Liam spoke. "I'm used to a lot more than this. Try keeping peace with Laycee and Leith when they get going. My mother used to have to actually put them in separate rooms. Neither would back down."

Ashling turned to her parents, giving each a quick hug and kiss and then headed for him. Tucking her hand under his arm, she turned him, speaking over her shoulder, "We're off. See you later. Just make sure Lorcan doesn't train Sally in any more words." Her parents' laughter spilled out the door behind them.

Liam closed the truck door behind her and then circled the front to his door. He stopped and looked around. Why did it feel like he was being watched? His eyes searched the area and saw nothing. He shrugged and shoved that feeling away from him.

Ashling watched as Liam's stood looking around. Her eyes went from him to the tree line behind their house. She had not said anything but she knew Teagan had alerted to someone there. She had seen an area or two where it looked as if someone had been standing for a while. A shiver ran down her spine. She did not like that feeling.

Once behind the wheel, Liam turned to her, watching her face. "We're off."

"And not to see the wizard, I should hope," Ashling responded.

Liam stared at her, caught her words and shouted with laughter. Her unexpected responses were just too cute. "No, hopefully not to see the wizard. How about Elmtown?"

She nodded and he pulled away. He didn't see the vehicle pull away from the curb and follow them.

"Leith," Laycee's voice came over the phone, a distressed note in it.

He stopped on his walk to the cafe and asked, "What's wrong?"

"Do you feel like someone has been in your house in the last few days, searching through?"

Leith paused. That's what had been bugging him, exactly that. He found items shifted from where he knew he had left them and shrugged them off as being tired, or that maybe Regan had moved something. "You know, I think I do. Have you?"

She gave a sigh and said, "I do. Joshua has the same feeling. He's calling Caleb now to come out and see. You may want to call too."

Leith's fingers came up to squeeze the bridge of his nose. He and Regan had planned to meet for a late breakfast and then head to Oak City for some time away. He guessed that wouldn't be happening now. "I will. Let me know what he says."

Regan headed to him from the direction of the cafe. She stopped in front of him, hands on his arms. "What's up?"

He pulled her into a hug and held tight. "Laycee just called. She thinks someone has been through her home. Joshua was calling Caleb."

Regan tightened her hug on her fiancee. "I know. I thought that about yours. I don't think mine has been but I'm in an apartment and Mr. Jones doesn't let anyone in the door unless he knows them or someone can vouch for them."

Leith looked down at Regan. "They could still find a way in. Ben told Liam it looked as if professionals had been in his place." He gazed towards the cafe and then sighed. "I guess breakfast at SueEllen's isn't happening today, is it?"

She shook her head and turned him back to his truck.

****

The Sergeants were on a mission. They were following Liam and Ashling. They needed to get close to them. The Major was putting the pressure on them. Whatever it was they had of the Colonel's, they needed to find it and fast. The Colonel would not suffer fools gladly, they knew.

They watched as the truck ahead of them turned into the parking lot of a small family-owned diner and the two occupants get out. They looked at each other and shrugged. They might as well go and eat too. They doubted they would be noticed.

****

Liam watched the woman sitting across from him. She had a natural physical beauty, but it was the beauty inside that drew him. She was studying the menu and then looked up to catch his eyes on her. She blushed slightly, set the menu down and propped her chin in her hands and looked back.

"So, this is how it's going to be today—you stare at me and me at you? Or do we get this out of the way now and go on with our day?" A mischievous smile crossed her face.

Liam laughed. "You caught me, I guess. Let's just say, we go on with our day. It's going to be an interesting one, that's for certain, with you, Ashling Downie."

Ashling smiled. She had made her point with humour and Liam had responded the same. Yes, it would be a good day.

They wandered through the small town, almost a village, for a while, and then headed for the nearby lake. The town was noted for having some well-planned walking and riding trails. Both were eager to see them.

Ashling stopped Liam with a hand on his arm and pointed. They stopped to watch the variety of ducks, and then their attention was drawn to some swans.

"I could watch those swans all day," Ashling commented. "They are just so peaceful."

Liam turned to study her. Her eyes were on the swans. He felt the same way about her. She had such a peaceful look on her face. Her eyes flickered to his brown ones and then back to the lake.

A small smile crept across her lips. "You really need to stop that, you know."

Liam grinned. "Stop what?"

She swatted his arm and moved away. "You know exactly what I mean. Men!"

Liam gave a shout of laughter and then ran to catch up with her. She tucked her hand into his arm and they continued. He liked the feel of that but would rather have been holding it.

Late that afternoon, they headed home. Both were tired, but the day had been wonderful. Liam's fingers tapped the wheel as he thought. He glanced over at Ashling. She had her head back on the head rest and was staring out the side window. He listened; she was humming slightly, content with herself, her company and the day. Liam smiled. It had been a good day. He had needed a day away from work and from all the stress at home. He needed to do this more, and just maybe, he had found a friend to escape with.

Lights caught his vision from behind. They were coming fast, almost too fast. He looked for somewhere to pull off. There was nowhere he could. Steady hands on the wheel, he kept his speed even. The lights pulled up behind him, way too close for his comfort. Then a second vehicle passed and pulled in front. This vehicle's brake lights came on. What was going on? Ashling looked at him, looked ahead and behind.

"Looks like we have a bit of a situation, doesn't it?"

"It does. Look, we're in our own area. Put in a call. I don't like this. Your door is locked?"

She nodded as she pulled out her phone. She had a really bad feeling about this as Liam was forced to a stop, boxed in front and back. This was not a good way to end their day.

Chapter 7

Regan stood with Laycee as she watched both Leith and Joshua talking with Caleb and Ben. There had really been someone through the two homes. It was subtle but it had happened. She shuddered. What if they had been home? Laycee reached for her hand and gripped it, replaying in her mind when her home had been invaded a year ago. At least this time, there was no damage but the feeling of violation was still here. She knew Leith would feel the same.

The two men parted from the Caleb and Ben and headed their way.

"What did they say, Leith?" Regan spoke first.

He shook his head. "There's not much, if any, evidence they can see. Someone was in and out very quickly."

He rubbed the back of his neck, then rested his hand on his black head of close-cropped curls. "Caleb figures it was professionals. Ben thinks it's the same ones who went through Liam's."

"Liam's!" Laycee's shocked voice cut through the silence his words had brought. Joshua's arms came around his wife and pulled her to him. "Why? What would we have of Liam's that they would want?"

Joshua rested his chin on his wife's dark head. "That's what we don't know. Someone apparently thinks Liam has something of theirs and because they didn't find it at his place, then maybe we have it. Caleb said he'd up the patrols here for a while."

Leith spoke. "Come on. I really don't feel like going in the house right now. Let's head for the cafe and at least get us a coffee. Maybe if we brainstorm, we might come up with something."

Caleb turned to watch the four drive away. He closed his eyes in a quick prayer for guidance and then turned to look at Leith's home.

Ben studied the area around them, an uncomfortable feeling niggling at him. "I feel like we have eyes on us, but I just can't see anything."

Caleb agreed. "I just don't get it. Liam has given neither one of them anything in the past month, not since before he was hurt. So who thinks he has and what is it?"

"I told you, Caleb. It's that Bradley thing. One can't get ahead of the other." He sobered at a thought. "I guess we'll have to track down Liam and find out what he has remembered. I'm not banking on much though."

Caleb thought about it and agreed. "No, I don't think he will. We searched that area and came up with nothing." He turned to his vehicle. "Let's take this up again in the morning."

Liam reached for Ashling's hand. She hadn't had a chance to finish her

77

call. His calloused hand grasped hers tightly.

"We don't know who they are. Just sit tight."

A light appeared at his window and blinded him. He heard a voice but didn't respond. His eyes moved to Ashling's side of the truck. A dark form was there as well. He shot a quick look at her. She was calm, a concerned look on her face, but not fright. He wished he had her calmness and peace.

Liam waited. He was not getting out of his truck. Glass shattered as the window behind his gave way. He ducked, pulling Ashling down with him. More shattering of glass and his door was pulled open. He turned. A gun was pointed at him and a hand was motioning him out. He hesitated and Ashling's door was yanked open and a gun pointed at her. Her eyes met his, scared but calm. He drew strength from her peace. Seat belts unclicked, they both climbed down.

No words were said as they were pushed towards the vehicles. Liam turned and reached for Ashling's hand, but she was pulled to the vehicle behind them. Prodding from behind forced him to walk to the truck in front, heart in mouth as he pondered what was happening. His thoughts focused on Ashling and her safety, he climbed in the truck. His hands were bound in front of him and then the trucks moved away. As he glanced back, he saw his truck following. There would be no leads, nothing to be followed. How was he to get away, find Ashling and get her to safety? He leaned his head back and closed his eyes in prayer. If this was how he had to get close to God, he would rather have done it a different way. God, where are You? Are you here? Why, God? He felt a whisper of peace envelop him. God was here. God knew where they were.

Ashling kept her gaze steady and calm. Her heart was racing inside her as she contemplated what was happening.

Who and why? She didn't know of anything in her past that would have led to this. It had to be something with Liam. Was it from his fall in the river? She had wondered if there was more to it than said, but no one had commented. Her thoughts turned to prayer and she turned her heart to her Father God.

The trucks slowed and then turned into a manufacturing complex. They headed for the very end. Waiting while a gate was unlocked, they then proceeded forward and into one of the buildings, the door shutting behind them. Liam thought it had the look of a garage but he couldn't be sure. Heart racing, he scanned the area, trying to find a way out but the lighting was too dim. He saw nothing. The trucks stopped and then a blindfold was clapped over his eyes. He was roughly pulled from the truck and then shoved forward and then shoved down into a chair. His hands were loosened and then pulled behind him and he was once more bound. He tried to hear Ashling but couldn't. There was just that silence. He hadn't been able to get a glimpse of the men, the lights had been too bright, and he knew they wore masks.

Ashling had been blindfolded as well and then shoved into a room. She stumbled as she was pushed and went down on one knee, her bound hands barely catching her as she fell. Who and what, she wondered again? Is it safe to remove my blindfold? She sank to the floor, head on her knees. The room was cold and felt dirty. She knew Liam was out there but was he safe?

Liam heard foot steps approaching him. The men waited, he couldn't tell how many, but he sensed at least three. Was he to find out why they had been kidnapped?

A hand grasped his head and pulled it back. He winced at the pain.

"You have something that I need. Tell me where it is." The gravelly voice sounded familiar, but he couldn't place it.

Liam shook his head. "I don't know what you want. I don't have it."

A hand slammed across his face and he blinked at the sudden pain, tasting blood on his lip. He shook his head. "I don't have anything you want."

The questioning continued. Liam's body finally sank forward as he lost consciousness. The Major looked at the other men.

"Put him in the room. We'll try again later. Meanwhile, have you searched his truck?"

One of them nodded. "It was clean. So were the houses we searched. What did he do with it?"

The Major stared across at the locked door. "I don't know and we had better find it and soon. The Colonel is getting very angry. You don't want to anger him."

Ashling raised her head at the sound of the lock being opened. She had removed her blindfold and managed to get out of her bonds. She drew a breath as Liam's body was carried through the door and roughly dropped on the floor. The door slammed and locked. Then there was silence.

Caleb raised his head from the never-ending paperwork on his desk at the tap at his door. Both Ben and Eddie were standing there and behind them, Leith and Joshua. He motioned them in and Ben closed the door behind them.

Keen eyes studied the other four. His heart sank as he realized it wasn't a social call. Something bad had happened and with those two here, it had to be to Liam.

"Liam didn't make it home last night. Ashling's mother called this morning. Ashling didn't either. That is not like them. They had planned to have dinner with her parents. She had waited, thinking they had decided differently or had had truck trouble. We can't reach either one on their phones." Leith's breath caught for a minute and then he stopped.

Caleb's eyes turned to Ben.

Ben responded. "We've put on an alert for them. Nothing yet. Lorcan's on duty and he had a pretty good idea where they were headed. Liam had been doing some digging on what Ashling liked to do on her time off."

Caleb shook his head. One part of him could not believe that the third Bradley sibling was involved in something like this. "Where are Laycee and Regan?"

Joshua spoke up. "They've gone out to the Downie's. They thought if they were together it might be best."

Eddie spoke up. "I'm headed to the town they were going to be at yesterday. I'll ask around and see what I can find." He headed for the door, hesitated and turned back, started to speak, then stopped. He looked at the ceiling and then back at each of the men. "I don't have to tell you, Leith and Joshua, and your girls, we'll do our best. We'll figure it out. Right now, you two need to be in prayer."

Caleb nodded as he left. "He's right. Now you two get back to the Downie's. We've got some planning to do to find them."

Leith stood, stature rigid. "I want to be part of it, Caleb. I won't sit on the sidelines and wait."

Caleb studied his friend. "Didn't think you would. But let us do what we need to do first. We can't go running off half-cocked without knowing where we're running to. Just be ready to go if we call. It's going to be hard but we need to keep things as normal as possible."

Ben watched as the two younger men walked away, despair and defeat in their demeanour. He turned to Caleb. "I don't know, Caleb. I just don't know. Something is off. I feel it."

Caleb searched for words. "I know, Ben, I know. I..." His words failed. He looked up to the ceiling. "Once again, we are going to have to trust in ways we never have before."

Ben nodded. "Unless Hannah has another one of her moments."

Caleb smiled. "I pray she does and quickly." His wife had been instrumental in providing the names of the ringleaders in both Laycee's and Leith's situations in the last year.

Ashling moved towards Liam's limp body. She reached out, her hand shaking, and felt for a pulse. He was alive. Her eyes closed in a prayer of thanks. The light was dim, the window dirty. She rolled him to his back and tears clouded her eyes as she looked at his battered face. Dear Lord, she prayed, please let him be okay. Please provide a way out for us. She felt him over. His ribs felt tender and when she pressed, he let out a groan. Bruised at least, she thought, if not worse. She tugged him towards the wall and then slid down, cradling his head on her knee. She wanted water to clean his face but there was none. A single tear dripped and fell and she angrily brushed at her eyes. Tears wouldn't help.

What were they after? Whatever it was, Liam had refused to give them. She bent her head over her friend and her thoughts turned to God. God, where are You, she cried? Why are we here? Please, dear Lord, protect us. Heal Liam. Let someone find us quickly. Her head sank back against the wall, strength spent. Her eyes slid closed and she slept.

A noise at the door roused her. It was daylight she could tell. A figure appeared, face masked, and set a paper bag down. Gray eyes met her and then the door was closed and locked. She leaned back and looked up. It hadn't been a dream after all. They really had been abducted.

She looked down at Liam. He was still unconscious. Whoever had questioned him had not spared him at all. Bruises and small cuts covered his face. Carefully sliding his head to the floor, she crept over to the bag and opened it.

Water and food. Apparently they were intended to live.

She pulled out one of the water bottles and reach for some of the paper napkins. She would have preferred a cloth but this would do. She returned to Liam and loosening the bottle cap, she dampened the napkins and brushed lightly at his face, removing dirt and blood. She cringed at the sight of his face. She then lifted his head enough to tilt the bottle to his mouth. She needed to get some fluid into him. He swallowed and then groaned, rolling to his side. His eyes flickered and slid shut. Ashling slid back to the floor and leaned against the wall. She had no appetite. Her eyes too slid shut and she slept.

Neither heard the door opening or saw the man standing watching them. He stepped towards them, distaste in his manner at the surroundings. He stood and watched them, then turned away. He would find out the information he needed, even if he had to kill them to do so.

He waited until the door was locked behind him, then turned to the Major. "Find what I want, then kill them." He strode away.

The Major stared after the Colonel, then back to the door. How was he to find out what the Colonel wanted? Liam had said nothing despite the beating. If he didn't talk, then how was he to find it? He had no stomach for hitting a woman. He didn't think the Sergeants did either. He paced, thinking. They had found nothing on their searches. Could it still be on the river bank? Or had it fallen into the river? If so, they would never find it. He had been sure it had been in his pocket and now it was gone.

Chapter 8

Eddie tapped at Caleb's door and then entered to find Ben there as well. Closing the door, he sat, exhaustion evident in his movements.

"What did you find, Eddie?" Caleb searched his face, knowing the answer before Eddie spoke.

"Nothing. I really didn't find anyone who remembered them being there. And I should have. Lorcan was adamant it was that town."

Caleb ran his hand through his hair. "We have nothing. No truck. No Liam. No Ashling. No ransom demand."

Ben nodded in agreement. "So what do we really have?"

A knock at his door stopped any further comments. It was Lorcan. He looked spent, and worried.

"Chief, I went back over the route they may have taken. I found this." He held up a bag with some bits of glass, then handed it to Caleb. "It's window glass."

Caleb studied it. "And you think it's from Liam's truck?"

Lorcan nodded. "I do. It's too fresh to have been there long. And I checked. We have had no reports of any vandalism or accidents in that area. It's a remote area, perfect for an ambush."

The three older men exchanged glances, then brought their eyes back to Lorcan. "Lorcan, do you have a dog ready that can track?"

Lorcan's head came up and he nodded. "Teagan. Ashling was working with her, teaching her to track. She wanted to make sure she knew what she was doing when she trained my dog."

"All right. It's too dark now but first thing in the morning, go with Eddie and search that area. See if you can find anything."

The next morning, Lorcan and Teagan searched the area. Caleb and Eddie watched.

"Ashling was here. I can tell by how the dog's reacting." Eddie turned to search the area. "I don't see that anything is disturbed along the road though."

Caleb turned as well. "No. It's like the two and Liam's truck just vanished into thin air." He sighed. "I've had enough of our people vanishing for days on end. Who is doing it this time?"

Eddie's eyes traced Lorcan's movements. "He's hurting. He needs to find his sister to make sure she's okay and he can't. The dog's hurting too. Ashling and that dog have a bond I have never seen before."

Caleb nodded. "I'm headed back to the office. Let me know if you find anything."

Lorcan approached Eddie, Teagan at his side but watchful, searching for her mistress.

"They were here, Eddie. They were here."

The anguished look on Lorcan's face tugged at Eddie. "I know, Lorcan. Nothing else other than the scent that stops and the bits of glass?"

Lorcan shook his head. "It's like someone reached down and plucked them away." He searched the area. "Now what? Where do we search? It could be a small area or a large area."

Eddie studied him. "You were involved in search in your previous department. Run me through the steps of how you started and if you searched in a wooded area, an urban area, an industrial area. All of those mean a different search pattern. Think it through. We'll head back to the office and you can be ready to tell me."

Liam stirred. He hurt all over again. His face was the worse. His hand shaking, he reached to feel. He didn't like what he felt. What had happened? And why was he lying on cold concrete?

He rolled to his back, groaning at the effort. His hand went to cradle his ribs. He couldn't tell if they were fractured or not but they hurt. A whisper of sound came to him. He just couldn't look, couldn't keep his eyes open.

He felt hands on his arms, his face, and then a soft voice.

"Liam."

He knew that voice and struggled to open his eyes again. He blinked to clear his vision and looked up.

Ashling knelt beside him, hand on his head. "Liam, you're awake. Thank goodness."

He blinked again and tried to speak. The hand left his head and then he felt it underneath, raising it up. Water touched his lips and he drank thirstily.

Ashling drew the water back after Liam had had some. She wouldn't let him drink a lot yet, it would make him sick.

"Do you think you can sit up?"

He nodded, then regretted it. "Give me a minute." His voice was raspy, his mouth and throat dry. Finally, he was able to raise himself up, Ashling's arm behind him to support him.

"If you can, slide backwards a bit. There's a wall there you can rest against." She helped him move backwards.

He closed his eyes, it had been such a struggle just to move. He drew in a deep breath, and then he felt her fingers around his, closing them on a bottle.

"Drink, but in sips and slowly only."

"Where are we?"

"In a locked room in that building they brought us to. It's been a day or so I think." Ashling looked around. "I've tried to find a way out but I can't. We're stuck. They did bring food and water. I won't touch the food but the water bottles seem okay." She slid down to sit beside him, her shoulder touching his.

"We'll get out, somehow." He reached for her hand and gripped it. "Where's your faith?"

Her head hit his shoulder and he thought he felt the dampness of tears. "It's there. It's just a dark spot right now."

There was the sound of the lock being turned and the door slid open. A figure stood there watching them. He stepped forward, face hidden. He motioned for them to stand. Liam groaned as he came upright and Ashling's arm slid around him. She pulled his arm over her shoulder, offering him support.

They were directed out into the large open area. Liam stumbled and almost fell, but caught himself. They watched the man as he motioned them, once again in silence, to the door at the far end of the building. They were motioned through and the sun blinded them for a minute. They stopped and turned. The man watched them, then pointed behind them. They turned. A vehicle sat there.

"Go," he said. "I can't let them kill you. That's what they're planning. Go. Godspeed." He turned and walked back into the building.

Liam stumbled as he turned. Ashling turned as well, studying the area around them.

"Come, Liam, let's go." She pulled him to the vehicle, helped to shove him onto the car seat, and then ran around the front. Keys were in the ignition and it started as soon as she turned the key. Cautiously driving around the building, she headed for the open gate and freedom.

"Please, God, keep us safe." She glanced at Liam. His head was back and eyes closed, pain evident on his battered face. "I don't know where we are, God, but You do. Drive for me. Guide my hands."

God answered. She soon found herself in familiar territory and headed for the hospital at home. Parking near the Emergency entrance, she ran for help. She knew she couldn't get Liam in on her own.

Caleb stood on the river bank, once more studying the area. Something puzzled him. Something had happened here, something that had almost cost a friend his life. He raised his eyes to the sky and prayed once more for wisdom and guidance. His phone ringing cut into his prayer. His eyes slid closed as he listened and then he turned to run for his vehicle. Liam and Ashling were safe.

Ben met him in the parking lot at the hospital, both intent on reaching their friends.

"Any word on what happened?"

Ben shook his head. "Not much. The doctors are with them right now. Eddie's been able to get Ashling's statement. Ashling said briefly that one of the men let them go and gave them a vehicle. She's worried about him. She was able to give Eddie an address. We haven't been able to question Liam yet."

"That's good. Let's hope we find some evidence there."

The waiting room held the family of both Liam and Ashling. Caleb ran his eyes over them and just thanked God that it was a hospital room and not a funeral home they were gathered in. It could have easily been one or the other. He touched Ben's shoulder, murmured a word and then headed back to the exam room. He spoke to the ward clerk and then turned to the room to his right.

Ashling sat on the stretcher, bracing herself with her arms. She looked up when he entered, blue eyes tired and strained. He could see the fatigue in her face.

"How are you, Ashling?"

She shrugged. "Alive. Out of that place. Ready to go home. Take your pick."

Caleb watched her. Her response was not typical for her. She was hurting in a way that he couldn't put a finger on. "Eddie got your statement." At her nod, he asked, "Have you thought of anything else?"

She shook her head. "No. How's Liam?"

"I haven't seen him yet. The doctor was with him."

She nodded, then as the nurse entered the room with her discharge papers, she said, "They hurt him bad, Caleb. I thought he was going to die." She raised her eyes and stared at him. "Find them."

Caleb nodded. "We will do our best."

She slid from the bed, staggered, then caught her balance. "Is your best good enough though?" Walking away from him, she left the room.

Caleb rubbed the back of his neck, having to agree that their best might not be enough. He went to find Liam.

Liam lay in an adjacent exam room, eyes closed, IV once again in his arm, this time with needed fluids and antibiotics. Caleb stopped beside the bed, hand resting on the raised bed side. He watched his friend's face and winced at what he had been through. Caleb doubted he had seen a beating like that for years. Eyes came up and he stared across the room. Liam wasn't ready to talk, but when he was, Caleb would be there. Anger began to burn within him.

Returning to the waiting room, he found Leith and Laycee. He spoke with them for a few minutes and then left. A hand touched his arm as he exited the hospital and he turned in surprise. Lachlan stood there.

"Let us know what we can do to help. We need to be doing something."

Caleb sighed. "Right now, pray. That is what we need."

Lachlan nodded. "That I can do." He walked away to where his wife and daughter stood.

Caleb watched them walk away. He had no idea who he was looking for.

Later that night, he stood at the entrance of the building and looked around. One more abandoned building used for nefarious activities. He turned and studied the outside, then stepped inside. Eddie came to meet him.

"What do we have?"

Eddie shook his head. "Not much. I would swear, if I was a swearing man, that someone knows exactly how to avoid leaving any evidence. We found where Liam was questioned, the room they were held in. Nothing else. Tire tracks aren't there, it's too dry to leave much of anything."

Caleb took a deep breath. "Why do I feel like we are always running behind? Do we have another leak?" He thought about how the secretary had betrayed them a few months ago.

"I hope not. We don't need that."

Chapter 9

Liam struggled to open his eyes. The pain was better and he couldn't figure out why. Then his vision cleared and he looked around. A nurse stood beside him adjusting an IV. He was in the hospital. He really hadn't dreamed it.

At his movement, the nurse looked over and then reached for his wrist. She smiled. "The doctor will be in shortly."

The door opened and a doctor he didn't recognize entered. He stopped by Liam's bed and studied the young man.

"I'm Dr. Adams. How are you feeling today?"

Liam eyes the doctor, who looked to be in his 40s. "I hurt. How am I supposed to feel?"

The doctor smiled. "Yes, you will for a few days. I don't know who did this to you, but they did a good job. Beside the bruises on your face, you've got some ribs there are bruised. Those will take some time to heal. The cuts on your face, I am assuming are from glass."

Liam thought for a moment, then cautiously nodded. "I think I remember the truck windows being broken."

Dr. Adams nodded. "That would explain it. It's mostly the left side of the face. Your clothing protected your neck and back and arm." He studied Liam's chart, then said, "I'm going to release you once the IV's finished and it looks like it almost it. You need to take it easy for a few days." At Liam's snort, he looked at him. "Yes, I know what you do for a living. You have men working for you. Let them do the work. You won't be doing much until those ribs heal anyway. And for the next few days, you'll not be on your own. Someone will need to be with you."

Liam glared at him, and Dr. Adams laughed. "I've met your family. How about your girlfriend's family?"

Liam's eyebrows raised in surprise. "Girlfriend."

Dr. Adams nodded. "Sure. She's been around a few times checking on you. If she wasn't, why would she?"

Liam closed his eyes. Ashling was fine. "Thank you, Dr. Adams. I was worried about her."

"Hold on to her, young man. She's a keeper."

Liam lay and watched the drip in the IV line. He wanted out of here. He wanted to find Ashling and see for himself she was fine.

The door opened again, and Leith and Laycee walked in. Laycee hugged her brother. Leith stopped at the end of the bed and watching Liam closely.

"Don't ask," Liam almost snapped. Both Laycee and Leith stared at him in surprise. That was not Liam. He never snapped at them. "And no, I'm not going to stay with either one of you. So don't even ask. It's not even up for debate."

Laycee looked at Leith, then back to her older brother. "But, Liam, you have to have someone with you."

He shook his head. "Not one of you. I'm a target and I won't put you there."

Laycee's eyes filled with tears as she stared at her brother, then turned and ran from the room. Leith watched her leave, then eyed his brother.

"Not debating it, brother. The only debate is which house, mine or yours."

"Leith, you don't understand. I can't put you at risk. If you're at risk, so is Regan."

Leith shook his head. "So, it's okay for you to pull the big brother card when it involves Laycee or me, but we can't pull the younger brother/sister card. Doesn't work that way. You're stuck

107

with me. Joshua would gladly have you there as well."

"I can't, Leith. They're newlyweds. I won't intrude."

"Then maybe you need to apologize to Laycee and tell her that. She'll understand."

Liam laid his head back. Leith was right. He did need to make things right with Laycee. He just wasn't thinking clearly.

"Go find her. She won't have gone far."

Leith left and found his sister. Liam was right. She was just outside the door. He stood looking at her until she raised tear-filled eyes to him.

"He's worried, Laycee. He's scared that you or I are going to get caught and hurt." He reached for his sister. "Come here." She clung to him as he hugged her.

"I'm so afraid, Leith. All I can think of is that I can't lose him. We almost lost you six months ago. He's been there for us always. When Momma died from her heart disease and Daddy from that work accident, he was there. He set his own grief aside for ours."

Leith felt her tears soaking his T-shirt. He laid his head on his sister's head and his own tears caught in her black curls. "I know, honey, I know. It hurts when he shoves us aside and he doesn't even realize he has. We just have to keep reminding him we're family and we're not going anywhere. We'll talk it out, we always do. Just keep those prayers going."

Laycee nodded, hugged her brother tight once more, and then stepped back. "I gather he sent you to find me?"

Leith stood, eyes on his sister's face, and hands on her shoulders. She looked so much like their mother. What advice would she give? What would their father tell them?

He nudged her towards the door. "Go, make your peace with him. Just remember, he's scared too, just won't show it. We have to let him have that. Just pray, honey, just pray. God is in control. Liam's been struggling since your episode last year. He's still the big brother, wanting to protect both of us."

Laycee nodded, swiped at her eyes, drew in a deep breath, and then pushed open the door to Liam's room. Liam looked up and then reached his hand for his sister. Leith watched through the slowly closing door as Liam caught his sister in his arms, looked up and mouthed his thanks.

Leith leaned back against the wall, emotionally drained. He so wanted to go in there too, but these two needed to work out what had happened between them. He wasn't needed. He looked up as someone stopped in front of him.

Caleb stood watching his friend. His heart hurt for him. The three had been through so much. Now the family was starting to show cracks. He lifted eyes and prayed for them, prayed for healing, for strength. He prayed for wisdom for his officers. They were at an impasse and without any further clues, they would not find out who was after Liam.

"It hurts, Caleb." Leith's soft voice broke into his prayers and his eyes returned to his friend.

"I know, Leith, I know. Come on, let's go get you a coffee and me a tea." He nodded at the door. "Laycee and Liam need this time. Your time with him will come."

****

The Colonel stood and watched, rage building within him. The fools had failed once again. What would it take for them to succeed? He needed that information. Did he have to take matters into his own hands. He glared at the door behind which Liam lay and then turned away to his tasks. Soon, he thought, soon I will have the information and you will be no more.

The Major watched the Colonel as he walked from the hospital and across the parking lot to his car. He knew time was limited for himself and the Sergeants. Which one of them had let them go and provided them a car? The Colonel had been in a rage when he found out. He now had to backtrack, pick up the pieces and make plans to find that information. If he only knew exactly what he was looking for, it would help.

****

Caleb sank into his desk chair and once again contemplated the files piled up his desk. He thought he had cleared it off last night but it was once again piled down. He sighed. He hoped to be out of here early tonight to spend time with his wife and boys. He wasn't sure if he would be able to.

A few hours later, a tap came at his door, and Ben and Eddie entered. He watched them.

"What do you have?"

Ben and Eddie exchanged a glance, then Ben spoke, "We've had a hit and run out near that industrial complex. The young man fits the description Ashling gave us."

Caleb thought, then nodded. "Of course we do. Another lead to follow. All right, run with it and see how far you get. We need to find these people and find them fast. Things are getting out of hand."

As they turned to leave, Caleb had a thought and stopped them.

"I know we've discussed this in the past. We need to start tracking who is prominent in the town who would have hidden access to what we're finding. There's something there, and no, Hannah has not come through with a name as yet." The two other men laughed and then left.

Caleb leaned back in his chair, deep in thought, pen rolling in his fingers. He nodded and then reached for the phone. He could help in a tangible way and he would.

A few hours later, Liam sat on the side of his hospital bed, trying to gather strength to get dressed. He had been discharged. Caleb had been by an hour or so ago and said he would make sure he had a ride. Strange, Leith hadn't been back. He was to go stay with him. Apparently, from what Leith said, Regan was already planning on mothering him, planning meals to tempt his appetite. Laycee and he had talked through what had happened. She understood he didn't want to intrude on Joshua and her. Leith and Regan was getting married in a couple of weeks and he didn't really want to intrude on their last few weeks as a couple before they married. That time was too precious for them.

A tap at the door brought his head up. Lachlan Downie entered and stood watching him.

Lachlan studied the younger man, taking in the evidence of his recent beating. He watched him, knowing his character. His daughter wouldn't say, but he could read her pretty well. This man, sitting on the bed in front of him, was becoming very important to her. He would do just about anything to keep him safe. His daughter had been hurt in the past and he didn't want to see that happen again.

"Liam." Lachlan spoke, then waited. Liam watched, wondering what was coming. "I've come to take you to our place. No, don't protest. Caitlin used to be a nurse until she retired a few years ago for personal reasons. With Lorcan as police officer, Caleb thinks you'll be fairly safe, about as safe as anywhere right now. You need a mother to look after you right now. You haven't had that in many years, I understand. Sometimes the strong one in the family, the protector, needs to step aside and be ministered too. Let us be your ministers." He looked up and grinned, looking very much like his son. "Besides, I have an added attraction at my house that Leith doesn't."

Liam's puzzled look made him laugh again. "Come on, Liam. Think about it. Ashling doesn't live at Leith's house. She's at mine."

Liam flushed, then laughed. "I guess we're going to have to have a talk at some point, aren't we, Lachlan? You've got a really special girl there."

Lachlan's head tilted and he watched the emotions flickering across his young friend's face. "We shall, my boy, we shall. She's pretty special in my opinion, and she needs someone pretty special in her life. You're that."

Liam looked up in surprise. When had his secret got out?

Lachlan laughed again. "Don't worry. You haven't given yourself away. Caitlin and I have been watching you and really haven't forgotten what young love is like. Now, let's get you ready and on the road."

Chapter 10

Ben stood at the side of the road, studying the area where the body had been found. There was't a lot of evidence that they could find. Whoever had done it had stopped and cleaned up after themselves, or else the hit and run had been elsewhere and the body dumped here.

He looked at the picture he had been given. A young man, late teens/early 20s. Someone's son who wouldn't be coming home. Eddie was right. He did match the description given by Ashling. He sighed. He would have to go talk with her and he really didn't want to tell her the young man who saved their lives was dead. It would hurt her, he knew.

He turned as Eddie approached. Eddie had managed to track down a name and address. This was one call they alway hated. They turned and walked to their vehicle. Someone would hurt today in a way they shouldn't have to.

Caleb accepted the cup of tea Caitlin handed him and sat at the table on their deck. Liam was there, drawings in front of him as he worked through projects he had upcoming and proposals he needed to submit. Work was helping, Caleb knew; it helped to keep the mind from thinking of what happened, at least during the day it did.

Lachlan and Caitlin joined them. They knew Caleb was not here in an official capacity but rather as a friend. Talk drifted through the messages they had been listening to at church.

A sudden squeal and then a shouted "Lorcan" startled both Liam and Caleb. They looked up and searched the yard, wondering what was going on. A glance at Lachlan and Caitlin showed smiles on their faces.

"Watch," Lachlan commented. "Lorcan has done something to Ashling. He won't get away with it."

As their gaze returned to the yard, they saw Lorcan running towards the outbuildings, Ashling at his heels. To their surprise, she tackled him and then sat on him, holding him down. Teagan danced around them, black and white fur glinting in the sun, barking. Lorchan's hands came up in surrender and after giving him a smack on the shoulder, Ashling stood. His left hand reached for her foot and she danced away, saying something to him. They heard a shout of laughter and Ashling darted towards the rocks at the back of the yard, Lorcan scrambling to his feet to follow. They could hear the laughter from the two before they settled on a large rock, shoulder to shoulder.

Caitlin laughed. "He never learns. It's been like this all their lives. He will torment her and then take off. He has never yet been able to outrun her."

Lachlan spoke up, laughter still in his voice. "She's taken part in marathons and half marathons. She's always been a runner. There have been few of her friends or teammates who have been able to catch her." He turned to Caleb with a sparkle in his eyes. "I don't know that Lorcan would want it known that his sister can still outrun him and beat him up."

Caleb shook his head. "I'll hold on to this. I may need insurance some day and it would be good to bring this up."

Liam's eyes were still trained on the two at the back of the yard, not saying anything. Caitlin and Lachlan exchanged a glance. He was seeing a different side to the woman they suspected he had come to love and it floored him. Their daughter had many sides to her personality and as she got to know someone, the sides came out.

Lorcan dropped into a chair by his mother and reached for a cup of tea and a scone.

"What did you do this time, Lorcan?"

He grinned. "Me? I didn't do anything."

Lachlan snorted, drawing the attention of the other two men. "Right, tell us that again."

Lorcan laughed. "I got her with the hose."

Caitlin looked at her son, shook her head as she stood. "I'd chase you too if you turned the hose on me." She dropped a kiss on his dark brown head. "Thank you, son. She needed that."

Liam's eyes turned from them to the woman sitting at the end of the yard. At a touch on his shoulder, he looked up. Caitlin stood behind him. "Go," she said softly. "She won't come to you."

Liam studied her, then stood hesitating, then headed for the stairs to the yard and Ashling. She looked up as he approached and then sat on the rock beside her.

Lorcan watched, then commented, "He's got it bad, that he does."

"And you will let her be, my boy." His father watched him until he looked. "Let her be."

Lorcan's face sobered and he nodded. "I'm off. I still have to find that dog for Ashling to look at."

Caleb turned the cup in his hands, his thoughts dark. He looked up to find Lachlan watching him.

"What do you know, Caleb? I know you're here as a friend, but you've moved ahead in the investigation."

Caleb nodded, his eyes once again going towards his friends. "I do. The young man who helped them escape? We found his body early this morning, a hit and run. It's too coincidental to it being an accident."

Lachlan's eyes slid closed. He worried for his daughter, for her friend. "You have identified him, I can tell from what you're not saying. Keep me updated, please."

Caleb stood, looking down at Lachlan. "I will, but keep watch. If either she or Liam remember anything, call me, Ben or Eddie."

Lachlan nodded, then spoke once again. "I find it interesting that you want one of the three of you called, not your dispatch. You are suspecting a leak somewhere. We will be in prayer."

Caleb's thoughts caught at how quickly Lachlan had picked up on that. He nodded. "Thank you."

The watcher in the trees stood so close, he could almost touch them. Thankfully, the dog had moved away or he would not be able to be so close. He watched to reach out and snatch them, take them somewhere he could find the information. As the dog returned, he stepped back and left. Soon, he thought, soon.

Teagan growled softly and faced the trees. Ashling reached down and soothed her, not realizing the danger that had lurked behind her. She turned to Liam.

He was watching her. "Did I really see you tackle your brother and take him down?"

She giggled. "You did. He can never beat me. It's been like since we were kids. He'd try and fail dramatically."

She sighed. "Liam, do you remember anything? I can only remember bits and pieces."

He shook his head. "You likely remember more than I do. But there is something. There was a voice that sounded so familiar, but I can't quite catch it. It's like the voice was out of the normal place I would expect to see him."

"You've lived here all your life. You know a lot of the people. It will come." She stood. "Come, I need to get to work, and you need to go relax. Doctor's orders and the nurse up there is watching for you to come relax."

He sat and watched her walk away, Teagan at her side. Lord, please keep her safe. I can't when I don't know who to protect her from.

He studied the ground around his feet. Something caught his eye and he bent over to pick it up. What was this doing here? And who had dropped it? He turned it over and over in his fingers. He needed to get it to Caleb. He searched the deck. Caleb had gone. He would call him or else Ben or Eddie.

The watcher in the trees had returned just in time to see Liam pocket something. What had he pocketed? Was it what they were looking for? He would have to find some way to find out. He slipped away. He needed to make plans.

The Colonel stood and watched the Major. He was failing him and he would need to be dealt with. Eyes then wandered to the house and the man walking towards it. Soon. Soon he would have his information and he would be free to leave this place.

Caleb stood at his kitchen sink, fingers absentmindedly tapping. He had been home in time to spend it with his boys. Hannah walked up beside him and wrapped her arms around him. He hugged her back, and they just stood, looking out at the darkening sky.

"You're worried in a way I haven't seen in a long time, Caleb."

"I am. It's this thing with Liam. I just don't get it."

He could feel her nod. "It will come. God will grant that to you."

He smiled. "What, no name yet?"

She slapped him and then moved away. "No, nothing concrete. Just impressions. It's coming." She stopped and turned to watch him. At her silence, he turned. "I think it is going to be another one of those unexpected names. What I am getting is that it is something who is well respected and a long-standing member of our community, once again." She sighed. "I just wish someone else would get these names."

Caleb reached for her and pulled her back into his arms once again. "I know, me too."

She rested her head against her husband and listened to his heart beat. "I just wish I knew now. I have a bad feeling."

Caleb sighed. "I do, too. Time is running and we can't stop it."

Chapter 11

Liam helped clear the lunch dishes and then turned. He was at a loss. Ashling had taken Teagan and disappeared earlier that day. He was healing but the ribs still wouldn't let him work out on the job site like he wanted to. He had caught up on his drawings, all the paperwork, and his secretary had told him to leave and go find something to do.

He turned as he heard Teagan and Ashling return. She smiled at him in greeting on the way by.

"Hey, Mam, Liam's bored. Let's send him to see Sally. She'll cheer him."

He heard Caitlin laugh as she headed to answer the front door. "That we should. He can teach her new words too."

Ashling came and stood near him. "If you're tired of holding up the counter, we could go find something to do. I have some puppies you can help socialize."

He eyed her. "They don't talk and flirt, do they?"

Ashling laughed. "No, but they would if they could." She stopped as she heard voices in the hall. She shot away from him towards them, and he heard the joy in her voice.

His heart dropped and he turned and walked outside. Why did he think he had a chance with her? Other than what they had gone through, did they really have anything in common?

During the afternoon, he hung around the outside of the group. He could tell Ashling and the four men around her age were good friends. He searched faces to see if she had an interest in any of them. None that he could tell.

Lorcan stopped beside him. He nodded at the group. "Don't worry. I can see you are. Ashling, Marc, Tim, Eric and Wayne and their wives have been friends since they were kids. They're a really close knit group. You don't recognize them, do you?" When Liam shook his head, he named a group that was popular in the area, singing music from the 50s and 60s. Liam's eyes shot to the group and then back to Lorcan. "You heard me right. I would hazard a guess, seeing as they're singing here at the festival this weekend, they're up to something."

Liam watched as Marc, he thought it was, handed Ashling what looked like a CD. She was shaking her head, laughing. The four men were doing their best to convince her. She turned, sought his eyes, and then turned back, giving a reluctant nod. Marc tucked his arm in hers and she laughed, again shaking her head. One of the others got down on his knees in begging position. She laughed again, pushed him, sending him backwards, and sending the other three into peals of laughter.

Lorcan slapped his shoulder. "Don't worry, brother. There's only one man here she has eyes for."

Liam hesitated, then walked back through the house. It was time he went home, he thought. He headed for his room and then packed his bag. He went to find Caitlin, thanked her and then left. Her eyes followed him, compassion in her gaze. He was hurting in ways that weren't physical.

Later that night, Caitlin tapped at her daughter's bedroom door, then entered. Ashling was curled up on her window seat, turning the CD over in her hands. She didn't look at her mother.

"What happened, Ashling?"

Ashling shrugged, then looked at her mother, tears in her eyes. "I don't know. The guys showed up and things changed. Lorcan said he told Liam that the guys, their wives and I had been friends for so long. When I looked,

Liam was gone. I didn't mean to exclude him. You know what those guys are like."

Her mother reached out to stroke her daughter's hair. "I know. You didn't exclude him. Right now, he's unsure how he feels about you or how you feel about him. It's all so new. Besides, you and he have been through a lot in the last few weeks and he feels it is not safe to be around you, if the danger is directed at him. He's torn." Caitlin stopped. "You also need to remember, he lost his parents when he was young, just in his early 20s. He had to grow up fast and be a father figure to Leith and Laycee. He's hurting, honey, and hurting in a way that only God can reach."

Tears sparkled in Ashling's eyes. "I know, Mam. I told him I saw that in him. I only wish I could help." She found herself in her mother's arms and hugged tight. She could feel her mother's lips moving against her hair in prayer.

When she pushed away, she searched her mother's face and nodded. She knew what she had to do, she just didn't know how or when.

"Get some sleep, honey." Her mother dropped a kiss on her head. She too knew what she had to do and tomorrow she would track down a certain young man.

The next morning, Caleb looked up as Eddie tapped at his door. Eddie entered, closed the door, and handed a file to Caleb. Caleb opened it, read the report, and then set the file down.

"Does anyone know beside you?"

Eddie shook his head. "I haven't seen Ben to tell him, but you're the only one.'

Caleb tapped his fingers on the closed file. "Let's follow up and see who his friends are. Someone has to know something about him. Andy Cole, let's see what you have to offer us."

Eddie left and Caleb settled back to his paperwork, then stopped. He knew the Coles, they ran just inside the law. They had never really been able to pin anything on them over the years. If this was the son, when did he cross that line?

He sat back in his chair, the leather creaking. Something was niggling at him, some connection to the Coles. He shook his head. It wasn't coming. He'd leave it sit and work away in the back of his mind. It would come.

****

The Major stood and walked toward the Sargeants. He was angry. He had the Colonel angry at him and the anger flowed through to these two men.

"You are fools. You really are. Did you think killing this young man would help?"

The Sergeants looked at each other. "He knew who we are and who you are. We don't know how he found out but he did. He's the one who let them go. We couldn't let him go to the police."

The Major stopped just short of them, fist raised and then lowered. If that was the case, then they couldn't have let him live. It was a shame. He had been a good source to get information for him. Now he would have to find another.

"Out!" He shouted at them. "Out. Go find that information we need. Do something right for a change."

He paced after they left. The Colonel was really coming down on him and he couldn't right what these two men had done. He stopped, staring into the distance. He had to come up with a plan quickly and fix what had gone wrong. But what?

****

Caitlin rang the door bell at Liam's house and waited. She knew he was at home. When he answered, surprised to see her, she entered.

"What a beautiful home you have." She looked around. "This is nice. You've kept to the period of the house with modern updates and touches."

Liam looked pleased. "I tried. Joshua really did an outstanding job. I haven't told him, but I have entered pictures into a renovation contest. I am hopeful that he wins. Leith worked his magic with the tile work."

Caitlin looked at the tile in the entry and nodded. "Both those young men are talented." She looked up at him, tucked her hand in his arm, and nodded. "Show me your kitchen. I understand it is really something to look at. And if you have a spare teabag, a cup of tea would be nice."

Liam looked down at her, then escorted her to his kitchen. She looked around at the off-white cabinetry, the beautiful porcelain tile flooring, the soft yellow, almost cream walls, the mottled brown countertop and colourful backsplash.

"This is really nice, Liam. You feel at home here."

"My mother used to say the kitchen was the heart of the home. Whenever anyone came it, it was the kitchen they came to." He set her cup of tea front of her and then sat beside her as she patted the table. "But you didn't come here to see my kitchen, did you?"

She studied the young man, wisdom gathered over the years teaching her to read him. She shook her head. "No. No, I didn't I guess. I came to see you."

At his surprised look, she nodded. "Right now, you need a mother. You are hurting, you feel lost. You don't know which way to turn or who to turn to. You need either your mother or your father and I am guessing you feel like a little boy lost."

Liam looked down, tears springing to his eyes as his friend read him so accurately. He nodded, unable to speak.

She reached for his hand and grasped it. "There will always be a part of everyone who needs their mother and their father. Fathers give protection, they give wisdom from a man's point of view.

137

If you need that, you have men in your life to provide that—Ben, Eddie, Lachlan, even men in your church. I would hazard a guess and say you really don't have a female in your life that you can talk to." He shook his head, and she continued, "Liam, look at me. Now, please look."

He raised his head and she studied him, then nodded. "I know how you feel about my daughter." Her grasp on his hand tightened. "Don't worry. Not many do. You are very cautious with your dealings with her and I thank you for that. She has a story that only she has the right to share with you and one day the time will be right for that. But for now, please think of me as another mother for you. Talk to me. Let me speak with you and pray with you."

At her words, something in Liam broke, something he had blocked up for many years. His head went down on his arms and he wept. He had been strong for so many years, not letting anyone other than his two siblings close, and even they didn't know all that he kept inside.

Caitlin let him weep, knowing he needed this. The crisis he was in right now was the catalyst to healing in his life. She finally stood and hugged him, her head on his like she would her own son. Her prayers for healing and strength resonated through him. When his tears stopped, she brought back a warm damp cloth and handed it to him. She stayed, talked with him, lead him to passages in the Bible she felt burdened to give him, and then prayed once more for him.

"Thank you, Caitlin. God knew I needed a mom today." He stood staring down at the mother of the woman he loved. He reached and hugged her. "Can I call you Mom?"

She laughed. "Of course. And if my daughter has anything to say, you'll be family." She stopped him. "No, I'm not saying anything else. I know my daughter and I am beginning to know you."

He closed the door after her and leaned on it. His heart felt lighter than it had, almost lighter than it had in years. He thanked God that Caitlin had felt led to come and talk with him. He whistled as he headed for his study. Now maybe he could work on that plan he had festering in the back of his mind.

He sat at his desk and reached for his pencil. His hand stopped and he instead reached for the object he had picked up at the Downie's. Instead of drawing, he rose and headed for his truck. He need to find Caleb or Ben or Eddie. Maybe they could figure out what this flash drive was all about.

Caleb entered SueEllen's diner and looked for Liam. He raised his hand at SueEllen's gesture with a mug and a piece of pie. She knew what he liked and would bring it to him. He looked around and saw Liam sitting in a booth at the back. Sliding in across from him, he studied him. Something had changed with him but he couldn't say what. He looked more peaceful, maybe. Liam would tell him at some point, he thought.

SueEllen set his tea and pie in front of him, topped up Liam's coffee and then left.

Liam sat, hands around his mug and stared out the window. He finally looked at his friend and saw the fatigue and tired lines in his face.

"You need a vacation."

Caleb snorted. "Like I'm going to get one?" He sipped his tea, then asked, "What's up? You wanted to meet and I don't think it was just for coffee."

Liam hesitated in a manner that was not like him. He finally reached into his shirt pocket for an object. He motioned for Caleb to hold out his hand and dropped it into his open hand.

Caleb looked at it and then peered at Liam. "What's this?"

Liam shrugged. "I don't know what's on it. I figured you'd have computer guys you could take a look at it." He stopped. "I found it near the rock formation I did at the Downie's. There should be no reason for it to be there. It was down into the dirt a bit, as if it was dropped and then stepped on." He paused again, his eyes once more searching the outside of the cafe, looking for what, he couldn't say.

Caleb waited, wondering where Liam was going with this. He knew if Liam suspected the Downie's then it would be very difficult for him to accept that.

"I asked Lorcan if they ever copied anything onto flash drives. He said no. They had a back up they used all the time and burnt copies onto disks. He said sometimes Ashling was given a flash drive by a band she friends with but it's a professional one and not this name. When we were sitting up on the rocks the other night, Teagan alerted to something in the trees behind us. Ashling didn't seem to catch that there was something wrong. I went back later and looked. Someone has been watching their home."

His brown eyes bored into Caleb's. "Someone has been watching them and not just recently. There is a spot that is well worn, I would say likely from before we started the work."

Caleb studied the flash drive in his hand, turning it over with his fingers. He nodded. "I'll have it checked out. It may be nothing or the break we've been looking for." He looked up at his friend. "How are you actually doing, Liam? I haven't had a chance to speak with you about all this."

Liam shrugged. "I'll be glad when you find the guys. Then I can go on with my life. Caitlin Downie stopped by today and we had a good talk. She has me pegged in a way only my own mother would."

Caleb nodded. "You need someone like that right now. Stay close to her and Lachlan." He then smirked. "It will give you a chance to stay close to another female in that house."

Liam looked at him and shook his head. "Now that sounds like something Leith would say."

Caleb stood, dropped money for his tea and pie on the tabletop, and hesitated. He laid a hand on his friend's shoulder. "We'll get it figured out, Liam, we'll get there."

Liam nodded and watched his friend walk away. He looked around. He still felt like he was being watched and he didn't like that feeling at all. He searched the faces in the cafe. A lot of them he knew, the others were tourists, he supposed. No one seemed particularly interested in him.

****

The Major watched through the window. Liam had given Caleb something and he wanted to know what it was. He couldn't see. He had a bad feeling things were about to get a lot worse for him.

The Colonel would not be happy if that was what he had been looking for.

He had no idea how he would ever retrieve it now.

Chapter 12

It was the day of the annual down town festival. Caleb was worried about Liam and Ashling. It would be a perfect day for something to happen. He had spoken with Ben, Eddie, and Lorcan. He would officers patrolling the down town but they always had lots of crowds. It had become a very popular tourist attraction.

Liam headed for the down town. He had hoped to take Ashling but she has asked to meet him there. He searched the crowds, not seeing her but finally seeing Lachlan and Caitlin. He headed for them and stood just behind them.

A popular group had stared playing music from decades ago. He could see some couples and lots of children dancing in the open area in front of the crowds. Strange that there was a roped off area. He wondered why. When he looked up, he recognized the group as the men who had stopped by the Downie's the other day.

He felt someone at his shoulders and looked. Lorcan stood there, scanning the crowds, eyes alert and not missing anything. He was on duty but had been asked to come in street cloths.

Lorcan shot a sidelong look at Liam. Ashling hadn't told him, obviously. He nudged him with his shoulder.

Liam looked at him.

"She really didn't tell you, did she?" At Liam's look, Lorcan laughed. "Well, I'm not about to spoil the surprise. It's coming."

Liam stared at him, then as the music changed beat, looked at the band. Lorcan laughed at again and shook his head.

Marc, if Liam remembered, spoke, "We found out after we were booked for this festival, that good friends had moved to this area. It took some persuading but we managed to convince one of them to join us today on stage or rather in front of the stage. For your pleasure, ladies and gentleman, Teagan and Ashling." He held his hand out and waited. "Um, Teagan and Ashling, you are out there aren't you? Ashling? Teagan?"

The crowds were laughing. Liam got a quick look of concern on Lorcan's face and then Lorcan laughed. Liam followed his gaze and his jaw dropped.

Ashling and Teagan ran out from the side of the stand and stopped. Ashling was dressed for the decade in pedal pushers, red sweater, sheer white kerchief on her neck, and a red sheer kerchief on the high ponytail she had drawn her hair back into. Liam wondered what was coming. Lorcan nudged him again.

"Watch. You'll enjoy this. It's something really different. She hasn't done this for a couple of years, last time with these guys."

He watched as she shook her finger at Marc, who laughed at something she said. She then positioned Teagan and started to walk away. Teagan crept along behind her. Ashling stopped turned, and hands on hips, spoke to Teagan, who crept backwards, head down as if in shame. The crowd shouted with laughter. Every time Ashling moved, Teagan moved. Finally, Ashling turned, Teagan stayed where she was, eyes intent on her mistress.

Marc spoke, "Teagan, are you finally ready?" At Teagan's bark, Ashling shrugged, said something to Marc, who again shouted with laughter. "All right, everyone, sit back and enjoy."

The drums started, then the other instruments. The men in the group broke into a melody of slower and more upbeat songs from decades ago. He could feel Lorcan moving to the music beside him, but his eyes were on Ashling and Teagan. He had never seen a program like that. Both moved to the music, with spins, sideway movements. Teagan would back through the legs as Ashling moved. At one point, Teagan was even on her back legs. He couldn't begin to describe it. It was amazing. The dog was actually dancing? What was with this family? A bird that talked and flirted and now a dog that danced?

Lorcan took a look at Liam's face and nodded. If Ashling hadn't had his heart before, she did now. He knew Ashling wasn't real comfortable out there, but her focus was on her dog and the music.

The music ended and the applause was thunderous. Marc motioned Ashling and Teagan to the stage with them, and standing with an arm around her shoulders, thanked her.

"And people, this lady and her dog live in your community. You have an amazing talent in this dog trainer. She also has an amazing voice. We tried to get her to join our band but she said we had too many years of friendship going for her to ruin our gig." He kissed her cheek and then let her go. Ashling and Teagan disappeared.

Liam's eyes sought for Ashling in the crowd. Then he felt a hand tuck under his arm and looked down. She was standing beside him, not looking at him. He could feel her swaying to the music. He watched until she looked up, and then smiled.

"You do hide a lot behind that beautiful face, don't you?" he asked.

She blushed, then nodded. "I wasn't sure I would be able to get out there, but Marc and the guys insisted. They were right. I've missed that." She looked up at him again. "It's not the first time we've done that as a group. We used to have fun when we were teenagers."

Liam reached and hugged her. She was surprised at first then hugged him back. Liam saw Lachlan and Caitlin watching them, smiling. Lachlan nodded. Caitlin searched his face and eyes and then nodding, let him know she was aware of how he was finding his peace and his way back.

Liam took her hand and led her away from the crowds in the square. They wandered for a while before he led them to a bench in a quiet area. He held out her cup of tea and waited until she sat. They sat in quiet for a while, then Liam spoke.

"That was quite the show, you and Teagan. Where is Teagan anyway?"

"Da and Mam took her home. They weren't staying."

"Your mom is quite the lady. Do you know she paid me a visit the other day?" When Ashling shook her head, he drew her close and left his arm around her shoulder. "She knew I needed my mom and offered to be my mom. She had such words of wisdom for me."

Ashling listened as he spoke about his conversation with her mother. She nodded when he finished. "She does have so much wisdom. So does Da."

She suddenly shivered and looked around. "I don't know, Liam. I feel like someone is watching us."

Liam was searching around them as well. "I feel the same. Come on. Let's go." He reached for her hand, but she tucked it into his arm instead. "Some day, you'll have to explain that to me."

"Explain what?"

"Why you don't let me hold your hand?"

"Oh, that."

"Yes, that."

"That." She tilted her head to look at him. "One day, maybe I will."

He smiled. "I'll hold you to that." He looked up. "That looks like trouble coming."

Eddie and Ben were headed their way, grim looks on their faces. Their eyes were scanning the crowds.

Ben spoke. "We've been looking for you two." He looked around. "We need to get you two away from here."

Liam and Ashling exchanged glances. What was happening?

Eddie spoke. "That flash drive you handed Caleb yesterday? We don't have a name, but it's got some really powerful names and money amounts. Looks like some blackmail going on, at the very least. If the blackmailer thinks you have it, he won't stop at anything to get it."

Liam's steps faltered. Blackmail! That's what this was all about?

"What flash drive?" He could hear Ashling's voice beside him.

"Liam found a flash drive near the rocks at the back of your property and yes, we know it doesn't belong to any one of you." Eddie's hand came up as Ashling went to protest. "Liam already knew that before he asked Lorcan if any of you used that type of flash drive."

Liam could feel her eyes on his and he looked down. A mixture of emotions were in them. He knew he would have to talk with her at some point.

Ben urged them forward. "We need to get you under cover somewhere. I'm afraid that whoever is after you has been here. I enjoyed seeing you and Teagan work this afternoon, Ashling, but it probably wasn't the wisest move."

Ashling stopped and faced Ben. "I refuse to live in fear. I will go on with my life. I know someone could very well have shot me today, but I'm not about to stop what I love to do because of that."

Liam turned his head and watched her. Her Irish temperament was showing. Okay, he thought, there can be sparks.

Ben and Eddie tucked them into Ben's car and they left.

"Where are we headed, Ben?" Liam asked.

"Right now, we're heading to your place for you to pack and then to Ashling's. We're working on a place."

"I hope it's safer than where you had Leith and Regan." When the two men winced, Liam flushed. "I'm sorry. That was uncalled for. I know you did your best but that leak."

"We'll find somewhere, Liam. We don't want to go through that again."

****

The Major stood at the bench. He had been so close. His sergeants were there too. They had just missed them. How did they always just miss them?

The Colonel was getting anxious and more angry by the day. He was losing patience, and the Major really didn't want to find out what happened when there was no more patience. He drifted away in the crowd. He would have to come up with an idea and fast on how to find them.

****

Ben's eyes constantly watched the traffic around him, searching for a tail, or something that seemed out of the ordinary. Eddie was monitoring the radio chatter.

Liam reached for Ashling's hand. Her fingers curled into his and tightened. He knew she was scared but it didn't show in her outward calm demeanour. He himself was angry, angry towards whoever it was that was stalking them. He had finally got to the point where he could think about his own life now that Laycee and Leith were settled.

His head went back. Leith and Regan—their wedding was in a few days. No matter what, he would be there, even if he had to ditch his guard and walk back from wherever they were headed. He would bring that up with Caleb when he spoke with him and speak with him he would.

Ashling was tired. She rested her head on Liam's arm. She had been fighting and running for a long time and it was time it stopped. Her eyes slid shut and her heart opened up to God. She just longed to rest under His wings and be whole again.

Leith and Laycee stood facing Caleb. He had asked them to meet him at the Downie's.   All had gathered in their living room.   Regan sat on the couch, watching, eyes moving from one to the other.   Joshua stood at the mantle, arms crossed, eyes not wavering from his wife.   Lorcan stood beside him, eyes on his parents.   Caitlin sat in her favourite armchair, Lachlan perched on the arm, holding his wife.

"Where are they, Caleb?"   Leith demanded.

Caleb shook his head.   "No, Leith. I won't tell you.   It's not safe for them and it's not safe for you.   You remember what you and Regan went through just six months ago."

Leith shook his head.   "Doesn't matter. I want to be there to help."

Caleb shook his head again, then let his eyes wander the room.   He saw the concern, the love on the faces of those gathered.   Hannah, he thought, I could really use a name. Please come through, honey, and soon.

"We are keeping it as quiet as we can. We have been given some information and in the process of tracking it down. It's really powerful and damning information. I won't take a chance on anyone's life." He stared around at the group. "Anyone's. Got me?"

They nodded. He then turned back to Leith.

"I know, Leith. He's your brother. You want to be with him, just like he did with you. I also know your wedding is coming up and you want him here to share these next few days with you. I will make arrangements for you to talk. And he will be here for what he needs to be. I know it's not the same, and this time can never be made up again."

Leith took a deep breath, then nodded. Caleb would do his best.

Chapter 13

Liam stood and looked around the bedroom of the house he had been taken to. It wasn't much to look at. He knew now how Leith felt last year. Please, God, he prayed. Let this end soon and well. I don't know if I could go through what Leith went through last year with Regan, almost losing her. Please, God, please hear my plea.

A tap at the door had him turning. Ben stood there, watching.

"I'm really sorry, Liam. I really hated to break up your day today."

Liam sighed, then sank to the bed. He motioned Ben to the chair. "I hated to have you do it. I just want to make sure Ashling safe. I hate that something directed at me has been brought to her."

Ben eyed his friend, trying to assess where he was at. Liam had learned to cover his feelings, partly from having had to head up his family so young.

He hesitated, then spoke. "Liam, you have borne a huge burden for the last 10 to 12 years. You have become a real man of God." He held up his hand as Liam went to protest. "You're struggling right now. I can see that. You hide it but those of us who know you see it. You have been the head of the home, the protector, the one who has watched out for your siblings in so many ways. Now, they are settled, Laycee married, Leith about to be, and you feel lost. That phase of your life is over and you really don't know where to turn. You are struggling to trust right now with what is going on. God understands. He is there wherever you turn. I can remember your father talking in a study group we were in not long before God called him home. He was talking about how God spreads His wings to cover us, that He shelters us. He provides a place to rest and refresh. That's where you are now. You need to do that. No matter what is going on for the next few days, that's where God is for you."

Liam looked at the floor, feeling rebuked. Ben was so right in what he said. He nodded.

Ben stood, placed his hand on Liam's head, hesitated as if to say more, then left. He closed the door behind him and rested his head back. Lord, he prayed, we're in that dark place before dawn. Be our light.

Ashling stood in the kitchen, assessing what was available for food. She was hungry and wanted food. She hadn't eaten earlier, being too nervous. She and Liam had planned on finding something at the festival but plans had changed. Now she needed to fix something. There was not a whole lot right now but she could make sandwiches, and checking the cupboard, soup. Not much but it would be filling. As long as there was tea to be had, she would be fine.

She turned. Eddie stood watching her.

"What?"

Eddie smiled. "Won't work, you know. The best have tried and it doesn't work."

"What doesn't work?"

"Wishing it was different. Wanting to leave. Please don't try and run. I can't run fast like you and I don't want to even try."

She studied him, then looked behind him at Ben. "I can't promise that, Eddie. I just can't. I trust you both but if it comes to protecting those I love, I will make the decisions I need to."

Eddied sighed. "Ashling, that's what I'm afraid of, that you'll make a decision and take off. If you do that, I can't protect you."

Ashling watched him, not seeing that Liam had entered the room as well as Ben. "Let me tell you something not many people know, other than my

163

family. You can verify with the police department where we last lived.

"When I was about 18, I had a stalker. It was brutal. I won't go into the details. It was a horrible, horrible time." She stopped, looking at the ceiling, tears shimmering in her eyes. She looked back at Eddie. "The police tried to protect me. It didn't work. I finally had to strike out on my own, away from my family. After about six weeks on the run, they finally tracked him down. He was within 30 minutes of finding me. He had threatened my parents, my brother, my friends. So don't tell what I will or won't do. My life is ultimately in my hands and God's." She brushed by him and headed for her bedroom.

Silence reigned in the kitchen after she left, shocked looks on the men's faces. They had not expected that. Ben spun to look down the hall, then back at Eddie and Liam. Liam sank to a chair, shock vibrating through him.

Ben turned away to take a call. It was Caleb. He stepped into the living room to have some space.

"How are they, Ben?"

"Quiet. Ready to fight us already. Ashling has as much as told us she'll run if she has to. Liam, he's not saying much but I know he's feeling the same. Just whether they run together or not." Ben hesitated, then asked, "Do you know Ashling's history at all?"

"That she had a stalker? I just found that out from her dad."

"I wasn't expecting to hear that." He paused at the window and looked out. "Now where do we stand with the flash drive?"

"I have someone working on it. Unfortunately it's going to take time and digging. I called a contact at the federal level. He's working on it as well since it looks as if there's federal crimes." Caleb stopped. "About Friday and Saturday. We need to get Liam back early on Friday. He needs to be with Leith. The wedding's on Saturday. I've had a number of men come and volunteer to do security. Their wedding is small and they opted to have a small dinner in the church hall. That helps. Makes it easier to control who gets in and out."

"That's good. I am gathering that Liam will want Ashling there. Can we work it out?"

Caleb thought and then agreed, he thought they should be able to.

"I'll call in the morning. Lorcan has already come to me, wanting in on his sister's security. I don't plan on that unless I have to. I don't want both Lachlan's and Caitlin's children in the line of fire."

"No. We don't. Has Hannah come up with a name yet?"

Caleb laughed softly. "No, and I wish she would."

****

The Colonel stood over the body of the one Sargeant. He had failed him. He

166

had tracked him down by following the Major without him knowing. This would be a warning to the Major and the other Sergeant.

The Major stood in shock, watching the Colonel. He had never expected him to appear and then to kill the man. It was up to him now to dispose of the body. He was angry as well. Thanks to the Colonel, he was down to one man and himself. What was he thinking?

The Colonel stared at him, then turned without a word. No word was needed.

****

Leith wrapped his arm around Regan and pulled her close. She could tell he was worried. She had no words for him. He didn't need them. He stared across the room at his sister and her husband. They were just as quiet, lost in their thoughts about their own race to survive.

167

Joshua looked up and caught Leith's eye. He shook his head slightly and Leith's eyes closed. Caleb wouldn't say where they were. He knew that. He had promised Liam would there on Friday and Saturday. He just wanted him here now. It wasn't fair. Regan's hand tightened on his and he looked down. Her eyes were on his and they had a peace in them he just wasn't feeling. He pulled her to her feet and walked with her to the door. He needed to take her home to her parents. Then he would come back to his place and spend the night in prayer. He would petition the heavens on his brother's behalf and also behalf of the woman he knew his brother loved.

Chapter 14

Two days later, Liam stood watching his brother, dressed in suit and tie, rose on his lapel, pace. He felt relief, his brother and sister were settled. His parents would be pleased at the life mates God had provided them. Now to get him through to the dinner and he just might survive.

Leith turned, watching his brother. "Liam."

Liam looked up, studying his brother's face and eyes.

"I just want to thank you. You've put up with a lot but you've stood in Dad's place so many times. I wouldn't be who I was if you hadn't."

Liam caught his brother in a hug, then stepped back. "Things will be different now. Our family has changed, it's grown. Come, let's get you out to your bride."

The wedding was small, just close friends and family. There was still sorrow in Regan's family after the deaths of an uncle and his son. Leith and Regan had not wanted a lot of fuss and bother.

They waved off the newlyweds. Liam sought out Ashling finally, his duties done. He could see Ben and Eddie headed their way. He wanted time with Ashling, time on their own. He held up his hand to the men, asking for five minutes. They stopped and Ben nodded.

He pulled Ashling with him into the chapel. She looked around.

"It was such a beautiful wedding. Regan was lovely."

Liam stood watching her, hands in his pockets. "It was. But she's not as lovely as what I am looking at right now."

Ashling refused to look at him. He moved to stand in front of her and when she wouldn't look up, he cradled her face in his hands and raised it so he could see. Tears sparkled in her eyes. One had escaped. He reached with his thumb and wiped it away.

"Don't cry, Ashling. You are beautiful to me." He pulled her into a hug. "I know we have to go back into hiding but soon, soon we can talk."

She shook her head. "I'm not going back into hiding. I refuse to."

Liam stood still, shocked at her words. "Ashling, please. Don't say that. If you don't, I won't either."

She shook her head again. "No."

He looked past her, Ben and Eddie standing at the doorway waiting. "Come on, precious one. We have to go."

She turned, resigned in the knowledge that she was leaving her family once again. She wasn't ready to, but she had no choice, not at the moment.

Caleb's phone rang as he was hanging up his suit coat. He pulled it out and answered it, a grave look coming across his face. This was not the news he had been hoping to hear. Another body. Another unknown. Another murder. Not in his town. Man in his depravity was wreaking havoc and he wanted it to stop.

"Okay, let me know what you find out."

Hannah stood watching him, compassion on her face. "Not another, Caleb."

He nodded and sank to the edge of the bed. "Another one. I'm so ready for this to be over."

Hannah sat beside him and took his hand, fingers turned to mingle with his. She had stood behind him all these years, supporting him. His sons sometimes complained that they didn't get to see their father as much as other boys did but in their young minds they knew why. He was keeping the town safe. She leaned against him and sighed. "I wish I had a name for you. This time I don't. Just the impressions I gave you before."

Caleb dropped a kiss on his wife's head. "It's okay, Hannah. I don't expect you to every time. It's nice when you do. I know you'll tell me if you do."

"Do you have to go out again tonight?"

"No, I don't think so. Eddie and Ben are covering the security detail. The other officers are working the murder scene. They'll let me know if I do." He looked down at her. "How about a movie night with pizza, popcorn, and my favourite girl?"

She looked up at him and smiled. "Sounds good, favourite fellow." Her smile dropped away and distress filled her eyes. "Oh, Caleb, I just got a name. I don't want to tell you."

He took in the look on her face. "Never be afraid, my dear, to ever tell me anything." He pulled her into a hug. When she whispered the name, his face paled and his eyes closed. Never would he have imagined that name. Now he would have to pull either Ben or Eddie back in to follow it up.

Ben closed his phone and went to find Eddie.

"Caleb called. Hannah gave him a name."

Eddie watched Ben's face. "Did he tell you who?"

"Not yet. He wants one of us back to the office to meet with him."

"You go. I'm fine with staying."

"You sure?" At Eddie's nod, he turned to the door. "I'll see if we can find someone to send out."

Caleb met Ben at the office and then closed the door. He sank wearily into his chair.

"I hate to put this to you this late at night, but I feel like we're running out of time." He studied the paperwork on his desk, hesitant to continue.

Ben watched him. "It must be pretty bad for you to be looking like that."

Caleb sighed. "It is. I can't even imagine the betrayal it's going to cause." He looked at his friend, studying his face. He said the name and Ben's eyes slid shut.

Ben shook his head and then looked at Caleb. "No, I wouldn't have expected that one." He sat for a moment, and then stood, fatigue showing in his movement. "I'll get started tonight and then catch a few hours of sleep. We're going to have to pull someone in to help Eddie."

Caleb nodded. "I know. With this, we can't work with just us three." He rubbed the back of his neck. "I really don't know who though."

"Lorcan."

Caleb shook his head. "He's too close. I'm not sure he could keep his perspective enough. They're really close."

"They are. That may be where the strength will be. But then again, if Lorcan disappears too, then they'll go after their parents."

"Let me think about it. I'll be here. That couch over there can be comfortable at times."

****

The Sergeant stood beside the Major.

"I've found them. I need to call in a favour and I'll have someone who can work with me. I'll bring them in. By this time tomorrow, they'll be in your hands."

"But will we have the information we want?"

He shrugged. "Maybe not, but he'll tell us where it is. You were sure he found something that day."

"If we can find it, then the Colonel will be happy. When he's happy, we're all happy."

Chapter 15

Caleb looked up as Ben entered his office. Ben looked as tired as he felt.

"We have another murder. No, not one of them." Ben sank into one of the chairs. "I just might not leave here. It's Paul Caswell."

"That's not a name I recognize."

Ben shook his head. "I have something digging into his background to see where he fits in."

Caleb sat back in his chair. "We need to end this and soon, Ben. I have a bad feeling."

Ben stood to leave. "I do too, Caleb. We need healing for our town. With this, we won't get that until it's all wrapped and who knows how long that will take."

Liam felt a hand on his arm and then his mouth. A voice in his ear was soft.

"Shh, Liam. Quiet. We need to leave." The hand was removed.

"What's going on?" He asked as he sat up.

"Eddie and Ben are talking. Ben's back. Whoever it is has found this place. They're trying to figure out how to get us out and keep us safe."

Liam's eyes searched the room in the early morning light. "We can't leave."

Ashling shook her head. "We have to. We're putting them at risk." She held up her hand. "I know, it's what they do for a living." She snuck a peek at the door. "I know where we can go. We'll be as safe there as here. Where's your wallet?"

"My wallet?"

"Yes. Take your driver's license out and all your money. Stuff that in your front jeans pocket."

When he hesitated, wondering what she was up to, she repeated it. He looked at her and then his wallet, finally moving to do what she had asked. She took his wallet and stuffed it into his knapsack.

"Ben and Eddie will make sure our stuff gets home."

She grabbed a beaten-up knapsack she had set on the floor by the window. She motioned him to her side as she carefully slid up the window. Once they were out of the room, she slid the window back down and then catching his hand, led the way to the open field at the back of the yard, then to the trees lining it. She stopped, staring back at the house.

Liam stood beside her, watching as well. "Okay. So's what the plan?"

Ashling smiled. "You'll never believe it I told you. Let's watch. Ben and Eddie will know soon and then they'll leave, making the ones after think we have moved to a new house."

Ben walked towards the bedrooms and listened. Silence. He tapped and then opened Ashling's door. The room was empty. A bad feeling came over him and he headed for Liam's. It was empty too.

"Eddie, they're gone."

"They can't be. How?"

Ben picked up a note Ashling had left, read it and then handed it to Eddie.

"That girl is scary." Eddie had to admire her. "It doesn't say where they're headed."

"No, she wouldn't put that down in writing." Ben sighed, then looked at Eddie. "Well, I guess that means we get to break the news to Caleb they're gone. It looks as if she has a plan she hasn't told anyone about. She did ask we make sure we take their stuff."

Caleb looked up at the tap at his door and stared. Ben and Eddie stood there but there was no Liam or Ashling. He beckoned them in. After closing the door behind them, Ben and Eddie sank into the chars in front of him. Caleb kept his eyes on them. Neither looked at him. Finally, Ben handed him a piece of paper.

Caleb took it and read it. He shook his head and re-read it. "You were there, and they still managed to get away?" At his nod, he threw the note on his desk, leaned back, throwing his hands in the air. "How are we to keep them safe when we can't even keep them in protective custody? How do I explain this to the families?"

Ben shook his head. "I don't know, Caleb. I really don't know. Ashling has a plan, I'm sure. She thinks things through, but it would have been nice if she had shared."

Eddie spoke up. "She wouldn't. She's not sure who she can trust right now." At Ben's protest, he held up his hand. "Yes, she knows she can trust us, but she thinks someone is leaking information. Considering no one knew where we were, it seems strange that car showed up just as we were leaving."

"What car?"

"An expensive one, with lots of power. They had covered the plates with mud so we couldn't read them. We didn't want to stay around, we wanted to make it look as if we were on the run."

Caleb just stared at the ceiling. What next, he wondered? God, are You in control and running this? Because I'm sure not.

He looked down at his desk and then at the two across from him. "Guess all we can do now is follow the leads we have and hope we solve this before something else happens."

The two men stood and headed for the door. Ben stopped and then looked back at Caleb. He went to say something, stopped and then headed out the door. Caleb watched him, wondering what he had been about to say. He sighed as the door closed behind them.

It felt like everything was spirally quickly out of control. He prayed that not one of his friends ended up as the next statistic.

****

The Sergeant stared around the house, moving from room to room. How had they gotten away again? Who was tipping them off? The Major would not be happy at all and he hated to hear what the Colonel would say. He was glad he had never met him and didn't have to. He was not looking forward to telling the Major those two had slipped through their hands again. Did they have a leak somewhere, had someone talked out of turn?

****

Liam followed Ashling as she made her way towards the down town area. He had no idea what she had in mind, but seeing as she seemed to know where she was going and why, he went along with her. She stopped near a rundown building and looked around.

"Come, Liam. In here." She pulled the door open just enough for them to enter and held it so it didn't slam shut. "Over here." She led the way to an area at the back that was dark and somewhat sheltered.

"I need you to stay here for me," she whispered. "I need to go get us some stuff. You'll be safe here."

Liam protested. "No, I need to come with you."

She shook her head as her fingers covered his mouth. "No. It's not safe if we both are out there. I can get in and out without a problem."

He stared at her, wondering how she knew she could. He studied her clear blue eyes. She was so sure she could. He didn't want to have anything happen to her.

He reached for her and pulled her to him. "I don't want you hurt."

"I won't be. I have friends here."

His hands slid down her arms and he pushed her back. "You have friends here?"

She nodded. "Trust me, Liam. I know who I can trust here."

He watched her face, eyes roving over it as if to memorize it. His hand came up to cup her cheek and he felt her lean into it. She shook her head and then moved away.

"Give me about an hour."

Liam sank to the floor and laid his head on his upraised knees. All he could do was pray. Somehow, he questioned if that was even enough right now.

An hour later, he heard a whisper of sound and raised his head. He tilted his head to listen. It didn't sound like Ashling's steps.

He stood and drew back into the shadows as much as he could. A form appeared in his line of sight, and he heard his name called. It was Ashling, but he would never have recognized her.

She had changed into scruffy sweat pants and a torn T-shirt. Dirty sneakers covered her bare feet and he saw there were holes in the shoes. Her face, arms and hands were filthy. But it was her hair that he couldn't believe.

He reached out a hand and touched it. Pink, blue, green and it was teased to look as it is hadn't been brushed in days. He wouldn't have recognized her. She had a pair of cheap sunglasses in her hand.

"What did you do?"

She grinned. "Didn't recognize me, did you?" She handed him some clothes. "These are yours. Go change and bring me back what you're wearing."

He looked at what she had handed him and then at her.

"They're clean. I was at the thrift shop. Don't worry. I wasn't recognized. Hurry, we need to get on the move."

Liam changed, feeling very uncomfortable in his new clothes: worn, holey jeans, stained sweatshirt, ball cap. He gathered up what he had been wearing, making sure to transfer his license and money. When he came back to Ashling was waiting, she studied him and then reached for a container she had.

"Bend down." He felt her rubbing something in his hair and then over his face and neck. He cringed.

"Be good, Liam. I know your mother told you to wash behind your ears. This time, you won't. It will help hide you." She finished running his hands and arms and when he looked all he saw was dirt.

He looked at her and went to say something when she grinned at him. "I found the cleanest dirt I could."

He shook his head and then took the ball cap she handed him. Pulling it down over his eyes, she studied him for a minute and then nodded.

"Okay, here are the rules. First, never look at anyone in the eyes. That's a threat. Next, keep your thoughts off your face and your face as blank as you can. Don't argue with anyone. That's a quick way to end up locked up. We don't want that. Don't stand straight, hunch over as much as you can."

He shook his head again. "Are you sure this will work?"

"It did for me when I ran away at 18. I know most of the people out there. I come here every month or so just to make sure they're okay." She looked around. "We need to go. Bring your clothes and we'll dump them in the box at the thrift store." She grinned at him again. "Sure I can't interest you in some hair colouring?"

"No. And I hope that's not permanent either."

"It's not. A few washings and it will be gone." She led the way to the door and cautiously opened it. "Come on. We'll get rid of this. I want to find Frankie."

"Who's Frankie?"

"He's a friend. I can trust him. He wouldn't squeal on us. He's been down on his luck and trying hard to get back on his feet." She looked around. "It may take us a while but we'll find him. I have word out I'm looking for him."

She stopped, then say, "My street name's Ember. You need to remember that. I need to come up with one for you." She thought for a minute. "Any suggestions?"

Liam studied her. "No. I'm never ever thought about changing my name."

"Trust me. You'll need another name. Your name is not that common. It would be easy to track."

As they walked through the down town area in the graying light, she pondered a name. Finally she looked at him and shook her head. "Nope, that one won't work, nor that one, nor that one."

He snickered. "Is it really that hard to come up with something to call me?"

She pushed him sideways and he stepped off the curb. "Yes, it is.

Nicknames mean something here." She shrugged. "I'll come up with something, or else Frankie will."

Chapter 16

Lorcan looked up as his mother stopped beside him. He was brushing Teagan, who was looking so forlorn. His mother's hand rested on his head and then she moved past to sit in one of the wicker chairs in the sunroom.

"Do you have any idea at all, Lorcan? Do you know where they are?"

He shook his head. "Ashling can be very wily when she wants to be. She's got street smarts about her that some of the average cops don't have. That's how she survived for those six weeks."

His mother laid her head back on the chair and closed her eyes. "I just wish I knew she was all right. It worries your Da and I."

"I know. Caleb, Ben, and Eddie are working on something, I know. They haven't said much but Caleb did mention that he might need my help."

Caitlin turned her head to study her son. So much like his father, just so much like her. He had a peace about him that she didn't feel herself.

"Did Ashling ever say much to you about those weeks?"

He sat back and thought. "No, she never really did. I know she said she had some good friends there she was concerned about but she lost contact with them. Do you know she goes down there every few weeks to make sure everyone's okay?"

"No, I didn't. It makes sense, though, knowing her."

Lorcan watched his mother. He could see the lines of stress on her face. He wished he knew where his sister was, but he could understand why she ran.

"If it had just been her, she would have stood and fought. She won't when someone else's life is at stake." He stood, crossed to his mother and hugged her. "I need to get going. I'm on duty soon."

It had been three days since Ashling and Liam went on the run. Liam's secretary was doing her best to run his office but things were piling up that only he could answer. Laycee tried to help but she really didn't know a lot about it. Leith was just back from his honeymoon (they had taken a long weekend and planned a longer trip once work had slowed a bit into the winter) and had his own work to look after but stopped by Liam's office to meet with Laycee.

"Liam gave you the power of attorneys, didn't he, Leith?"

Leith nodded. "But I don't think this is what he had in mind when he did that." He stopped. "I just wish I knew where they were."

"Me, too. Joshua and I were talking about that this morning. If we knew for sure they were safe, we'd be okay."

Liam's secretary appeared at the door. "Liam said a while ago that he had wanted to slow down this fall a bit. Did he mention that to you?" When they shook their heads, she hesitated. "I just don't know. Bud keeps pushing for more work, but Liam wasn't budging on increasing the work load. We can't go ahead with new jobs without Liam's input."

Leith watched her. "No, we'll let it go for a week or so and then consider what we need to do. Hopefully by that time, Liam will be home." He stood and looked over to Laycee. "I have an errand to run. Will you be okay here?" At her nod, he left.

Caleb looked up at the knock at his door. Leith and Joshua stood there. He beckoned them in and Joshua closed the door. He sat, just watching and waiting.

Leith spoke. "What's going on, Caleb? Do you know where they are?"

Caleb shook his head. "Wherever they are, they're safe. I haven't seen any reports about them. They both have good heads on their shoulders. I know, I know. They ran from protective custody. They shouldn't have, but they did."

Leith looked down at his hands. "I need to make some decisions about Liam's work. I just don't know what to do."

Caleb spoke slowly. "I would hold out for as long as you can. Liam's got a good reputation; his customers are understanding."

Leith nodded, started to say something, then stopped. He gave a half smile. "I now know how Liam felt. I don't like it." He stood and walked from the room.

Caleb looked after him, then at his own brother. "Stick close to him, Joshua. There are things happening I can't talk about but it is really going to hurt that family and this town."

Liam sank down to the sidewalk. He was exhausted. This was worse than putting in a long heavy day at his work. He leaned his head back against the building. He just wanted to go home, to get clean, and sleep.

Ashling sat down besides him, her head going to his shoulder. She was exhausted as well. She had managed to track down Frankie, a friend on the street, and he was out looking for information for her. Hopefully he would find out something. He said he had bits and pieces but wanted to put it all together.

"Did you think we'd be here this long?" Liam's voice was tired.

He felt her head shake. "No, I thought a day, but Frankie's good. If anyone can find out what we need, he will. He'll pass it on to Ben or Eddie for me." He felt her smile. "How do you like your street name?"

He snorted. "Who in their right mind calls me Eagle?"

196

"That's what you are, my friend. Frankie sees into people in a way most people don't."

"Why Ember for you?"

She shrugged. "Part was a play on my name. Another part, he said I had a spark about me he didn't see much. He comes up with a lot of the names for his people here." Her voice trailed away, and Liam felt her relax. He wasn't comfortable out here in the open like this, but he didn't think too many of their friends would recognize them.

He watched as she slept, watched those around, watched for those who might come. He knew he was falling in love with this lady and he didn't want harm to come to her.

Frankie dropped down on his other side, then peeked at Ashling. "She's running on nerve. She can't keep going."

"I know. I just want to get her home. She got involved just by being my friend."

"That's not what she tells me. She tells me you got into trouble, she helped out, and now she's stuck with you. I say it goes both way. You're both stuck with one another. Take care of her, Eagle, or you'll answer to me." Frankie stopped talking and just watched. "Tell her I passed the information on like she wanted me to." He got up and left.

Ashling stirred, then looked after Frankie. "I knew he would come through."

Liam let out a quiet laugh. "You were faking it, and Frankie knew it. Hopefully, whatever he passed on will be enough to let us get home."

"I hope so too." Ashling stood, then reached for his hand. "Come on, it's almost time for supper at the shelter. Maybe tonight we'll be able to get some cots and sleep indoors for a change."

Ben went looking for Caleb and found him at the photocopier. He handed him a mug of tea and then waited. Caleb looked up, the fatigue and strain evident in his face. He nodded and then grabbed the copies he had been making.

Once in Caleb's office, Ben handed him a dirty envelope. Caleb opened it and began to read. His eyes slid shut. Ashling and Liam were safe.

"We were right. She did run to the streets."

Ben nodded. "I know who that is who passed that on. He feels like he owes Ashling. He'll keep her as safe as he can and as long as Liam stays with her, he'll be fine. She has made a real difference in lives down there. I never knew how much until now."

"I didn't know she was down there that much."

"With the information Frankie has found, where do we go?"

"More digging, my friend, more digging. He has really done a lot of leg work for us in such a short time."

"He has." Ben stood. "I'll keep digging from my end. Maybe we'll meet somewhere in the middle."

Caleb blew out a breath and knew he needed to meet with the families for an update. He couldn't share much but at least he could let them know Ashling and Liam were alive and well.

****

The Sergeant stood in the down town area. He had searched so many areas of the town. This was one area he hadn't and he really didn't want to be here. He had no use for the people who lived on the streets. As far as he was concerned, they were losers. He looked around. He had heard rumours that those two were here, but no matter how much of a reward he offered, no one would tell him what he wanted to know. He would keep searching, hoping to find someone desperate enough to want his money.

****

Caleb had met with the families. He could offer little for their comfort, other than the two were alive and safe. He entered his home, soft lights filling the downstairs. Once again, he was too late to spend time with his boys.

Hannah came into the kitchen as he dropped into a chair. She moved to make him a cup of tea and heat some dinner for him. He felt almost too tired to eat but knew he had to. Talking quietly as he ate, they discussed the day's events in each of their lives, then joining hands, bowed their heads to raise their friends to the Heavenly Father.

Chapter 17

"We've found them."

The Major closed his eyes in relief. Now maybe the Colonel would back off and let them find the information he wanted.

"Where?"

"They're in the down town area somewhere. They keep on the move but someone saw him. There was a girl with him but they couldn't be sure if it was her."

"Find them. We'll deal with them once you have them."

"Give me a day at the most."

****

Liam stood watching the crowds, tense. He had had a feeling all day he was being watched but couldn't pinpoint a face. They had been found, somehow. He turned to find Ashling. He reached for her hand and pulled her with him.

"We need to go."

Her eyes flew to his. "Where are they?"

"I don't know but they're out there. Where can we go?"

Ashling's eyes flew around the area. She knew if she asked, her friends would help, but she didn't want to ask them to risk their lives, and she knew that's what would happen.

"Come, let's head that way. Keep your head down. Wait." She looked around, darted away and then came back. "Here, put this on instead of the ball cap." She handed him a battered straw hat. "If they've seen you in the cap, this might just give us a chance to get ahead of them."

Liam caught her hand and led her slowly through the crowds, head down, but eyes watchful. He tried to shuffle as he had seen those do who really had no hope did.

Ashling searched for somewhere they could hide, but where? Where would they really be safe? Did they go back to Caleb? They couldn't go to their families, that might be their deaths.

God, she cried, where are You? Where do we run?

Liam pulled her hand. They headed down a small alleyway, trying doors. He pulled one open and shoved her inside

"I'm going to try and block it somehow. If I can, we'll try for the other door and leave that way. We need to get away from this area."

Ashling stood and watched as he jammed the door, He grabbed his hand and pulled her forward to the end of the building. He cracked the door. They were safe so far. They ran for the end of the alley, then towards the edge of town.

"There!" Ashling pointed at a derelict building. "In there. I know there are hiding places in there they would never think of." She led him in and away from the doors. How she knew of these places, he wouldn't ask now but one day he would.

The men following them stopped and stared around. Where had they gone? They couldn't have gotten away again. They looked at each other and then one pointed to a building. Just maybe that one. They took off on a run towards it.

Caleb met Ben and Eddie at the edge of the down town area. They were on a search for Liam and Ashling. It was crucial that they found them and found them today. Word had come from the street that a contract was out to bring them in to the Colonel and it really didn't matter what condition they were in, as long as they could still speak. Caleb had a piece of paper tucked in his pocket. He had been devastated when Hannah handed it to him. After all these years, he still didn't understand the way God worked through her, to provide names for him. He hadn't shared it yet with the two beside him.

Ben and Eddie's eyes scanned the area as well. It was a busy day down town with the local farmer's market and the annual artisan's market. How would they ever find them?

A voice spoke to their right. "Don't look. I know where they are. Head for the old electric building." The voice stopped and the man slid away through the crowd.

"Frankie." Ben was sure that was who it was.

Caleb nodded. "We need to split up and make our way there one at a time. We have enough men around here out of uniform if and when we need them. Ben, find Frankie. He knows more than what he said."

One by one, they disappeared into the crowd. They were leisurely in their walk, not in any hurry to get there. Eyes scanned the crowds for the one man they had confirmed was involved but they couldn't see him. If he was there, the crowds hid him well.

Ben stopped at a bench and sat for a minute. A hunched figure in tattered clothes sat there already. Ben handed over a cup of coffee he had purchased just for that reason.

Frankie peered out from under his hat. "They're hiding. The ones after them? They're getting close. Someone gave them up to him."

Ben didn't acknowledge that Frankie had spoken. It was an unwritten understanding that he didn't. "Do you have names?"

"Yes." Frankie repeated names to Ben.

Ben's eyes slid shut. Caleb was right. It was really going to hurt when they had to make those arrests. He stood and stared down at Frankie. "Go on," he said in a loud voice. "Move on before I arrest you."

Cowering, Frankie moved away, until he was lost in the crowd, then straightened up and headed for the abandoned building at the edge of town. Ashling was a good friend. He needed to help her. Her friend, Liam, he was still not sure about him, but Ashling seemed to like him, and like him a lot. So if she liked him (and he knew she read people very well), then he would help keep him alive.

Liam sank to the floor and tried to catch his breath. He was done running. He wanted his life back. He was ready to go to Caleb again. He paused, thinking of Ashling. She had pushed him back here and then disappeared again. His eyes slid closed as he prayed for her safety.

A small noise reached his ear and he tensed. It was Ashling.

"I think we're okay here for now." Her voice was low as she spoke near his ear. "There's an opening wide enough for us to get out if we have to just behind that tank."

"How do you know all this?" Liam stared at her in the gloom. She was tired, dirty, and unkempt but still very beautiful to him.

She shrugged. "Friends tell me. My friends here on the street? They find these places. There are times when they need to escape and have a whole system of hideouts."

Liam shook his head. "Ashling, what am I do to with you?"

She gave a soft laugh. "If you don't know, then who am I to tell you?" She stopped. "Shhh. There's someone out there. Be prepared to move."

Ben stopped by Caleb. He watched his friend's face. He saw the fatigue and stress in it, but he could see there was more than that.

He spoke. "Frankie came through again."

Caleb nodded and waited for Ben to speak. Ben seemed to be having difficulty with his words. Caleb had a good idea why.

"He gave me a name." Ben looked up at the bright blue sky. "I suspect Hannah has already told you, I can tell." Ben paused. "Why do people have to be like that? Why destroy what you have built up? Why damage people so badly? Who would ever of thought of that name?"

Caleb spoke, "You're right. Hannah did give me that name. It's really going to tear through our community, more so than with the other two." He hesitated, then spoke, "Man's depravity and sin sometimes just overwhelms us. If I didn't have God, I don't know if I could continue in this line of work."

Ben nodded. "Let's go find Eddie and break the news to him."

The two men moved off.

****

The Major followed after his Sargeants. Where were they headed? Had they found them? The Colonel was getting very anxious and angry. He just wished he had never gotten involved with him. Maybe he should just cut his losses and run, but where would he run to? He was in way too deep now to do that. He sighed. It was not what he had envisioned when he was approached by the Colonel.

Chapter 18

Ashling drew closer to Liam. They could hear voices and footsteps in the large open area of the building. Debris was kicked. She grasped his hand tightly, prepared to move. They knew the building was being searched and they could hear the searchers coming closer. Then the footsteps moved away to another section of the building. Ashling pulled at Liam and motioned to the back of the building. They rose as quietly as they could and made for it.

"You're not going anywhere, my friends." A voice spoke behind them. "You're coming with us."

Liam didn't look around to see if the speaker was in the room where they had hidden. He pushed Ashling ahead of him towards the opening and prayed that they made it safely. A shot pinged off the tank ahead of them and they dropped to the floor. Steps sounded behind them once again

"On your feet, you two. We've places to go and people to see."

Liam pulled himself to his feet and helped Ashling up. His heart sunk. All this time, they had been safe and now they were once again in the hands of their hunters. He took a quick look at Ashling. Her face was calm, serene, how he wondered. Her eyes were staring at the men, but he could see that she was thinking about how to get away.

They were roughly pulled from that room and then shoved towards the door. The men no longer bothered to cover their faces, as if they knew Liam and Ashling would never live to identify them. Liam started when he recognized the two who held them. How had they sunk so low?

Another figure appeared in the sunlight streaming towards them. Liam vaguely recognized the man, but his mind refused to believe it was who he thought. He shook his head.

A shove from behind sent Ashling to her knees. Liam spun, ready to fight for the woman he loved, then his hands went up in the air as the revolver pointed at him cocked, ready to fire. He wouldn't be able to help her if he was injured or dead. He reached for her hand once again, in defiance of the men holding them.

The Major spoke. "Well done. Now, let's get out of here before the police get here. The Colonel is waiting."

Liam's head jerked towards the speaker. It was really who he thought, a friend, someone he thought he knew and trusted.

Once outside, they were shoved roughly into the back seat of an SUV. Liam grasped Ashling's hand. She was calm and he wondered how she could be. His eyes darted around, looking for a way out and not seeing one.

A curse came from the driver. "What are they doing?" The horn honked as people started to mingle around the vehicle, keeping it from moving forward.

Hands reached for the doors and pulled them open. The three men were shouting, the driver trying to inch forward.

Liam felt a hand on his arm and he was jerked from the vehicle. Ashling followed, holding tight to his hand. They disappeared in the crowd. They could hear the shouts and curses from the vehicle. Ashling's friends slowly moved away. They had returned her love and friendship to them in such a tangible way, Liam was awestruck.

Frankie appeared and motioned for them to follow him. He led them to another building, this time at the other end of town. When they were safe inside, he stopped and studied them.

"You tried, Ember, you tried. You and the Eagle almost made it."

She nodded. "Now what, Frankie? Where do we go? If they found us once they'll find us again."

He pursed his lips as he thought. "Yes indeed they will. However," he held up a finger, "I might just have a plan. Are you prepared to go back into custody again?"

Liam watched him closely. There was something different about him right now, but he wasn't sure what.

Ashling was shaking her head. "No. I don't trust everyone in the department. I think someone gave us away."

"Someone did. And I know who. Stay here. I'll be back at dark."

Ashling watched him leave, then turned to look around the building. "Liam, I don't like this place. I don't feel safe here. I trust Frankie, but something isn't right."

Liam caught her close in a hug. "I know. Something seems different about

216

Frankie right now. I think we should try to find a place on our own. But where?"

Ashling hugged Liam back. She was filthy, exhausted, hungry, yet Liam made her feel like the most beautiful woman on earth. She could get used to that.

She turned and wandered through the building. She came back to where Liam stood. "I don't like this building. It's unsafe. Do you know what they used to make here?"

Liam had to think. The building had been abandoned for years. "I can't remember off hand, but it was something in the manufacturing field." He spoke as he walked through the building. "It will come, but I think it was…" He shook his head. "No, it's not coming to me right now."

Caleb looked around at the building. "They were here. From the dirt, it looks as if they were taken out and not willingly."

Ben shook his head. "No, they weren't." He took a deep breath. "But where are they? I heard that a large group of people stopped a SUV. Wonder if they got away?"

Caleb gave a brief laugh. "I can bet Frankie had something to do with that. Has Eddie been able to track him down?"

"He was trying to, but you know Frankie. If he doesn't want to be found, he won't be."

Caleb nodded and then was lost in thought. "If you wanted to hide someone, where would you take them?"

Ben pondered that a for a few minutes, then turned and walked out the door. Caleb followed. Ben knew this town, knew where the hiding places were, which buildings were best.

"I've got it. I just hope we're in time." Ben headed off at a run, Caleb at his heels.

Eddie was coming towards them. "I found them, but so have the others.

I'm not sure who will get there first, us or them. I put in a call for back up."

"Which building?"

"The old mill."

Fear shot through the three men. They had to get there before the others. Dodging through the crowded streets, they headed for the mill.

Ashling took another walk through the building, studying it. She didn't like it at all.

"Liam, was this a mill, by chance?"

He spun. "It was. I have heard lately that it has been used at times for drugs. I don't like this." He reached for her hand and pulled. "Come on, we're out of here."

Liam reached for the door and then stopped as it opened. Here we go again, he thought.

Ben stood in front of him. "Don't you think it's time you two stopped running? You've certainly led us on a merry chase."

"That's what makes life interesting, Ben." Ashling stood just behind Liam. "Life's boring otherwise."

Ben just stared at her. "Ashling, we don't need this kind of interesting. We know who we're after now. We just need to keep you two safe until we can arrest them.:

Liam could feel Ashling shaking her head. "No, Ben, you can't. There is someone who is leaking information on us. I just haven't figured out who yet."

Caleb spoke as he entered the building. "We do. Steps are being taken to prevent that person from contacting anyone." He studied the two. "I must say, though, you two have been very creative in how you hid."

Liam shook his head. "It wasn't me, it was her."

Caleb closed his eyes, drew in a deep breath, and then said, "Come, let's get out of here."

Eddie shot through the door. "They've found them. I can see them coming."

Caleb sighed. "Somehow, I just knew that would be the case."

Liam spoke up. "I know who they are."

Caleb looked back at him. "I know. So do we and we know who is paying them. We just need to get you out of here."

"Where's the back door?"

"It's blocked. This is the only way out, unless we go up and out the top door, and there's no guarantee the stairs are safe. I was through here a few weeks ago with that drug sweep we had." Eddie looked around.

"We're not trapped." Ashling looked confident.

"Yes, we are." Liam argued. "Didn't you hear what they said?"

"Sure, but they don't know the secrets my friends have shared. Keep watch and I'll be right back."

As she turned, Caleb caught her arm and stopped her. "Eddie or Ben will go with you."

She huffed and then agreed. "Come on, whichever one of you it is. I can show you an opening that we can get out of."

Eddie was on her heels and then came back. "She's right. There's an opening and I don't think they've found it. They know there's only one door that you can get in and out of."

Chapter 19

Caleb heard a shout of "There they go" as they ran from the building. He could hear the sound of gunfire behind them. They reached shelter and paused, Caleb staring behind them.

"Ben, we need these two out of here now"

"I know. It looks like they've trapped us though." He slanted a look at Ashling. "Any new ideas?"

She shook her head. "I think you've had them all."

Liam spoke up. "Now what?"

Eddie took a look around. "Over there. If we can make it, we should be able to get away. That gunfire is going to attract a lot of attention." Sirens could be heard nearing the downtown.

Caleb took a look, and then shoved Ashling and Liam. "Go, we'll cover you."

Ashling and Liam took off running, Eddie on their heels, Ben and Caleb staying behind to provide a cover. They turned as they heard a cry and saw Caleb go down and Ben reach and pull him back to cover. Eddie pushed at them.

"Keep moving. Ben'll look after Caleb. They don't want them, it's you two that we need to get to safety."

They ran for the next building and then slid to a halt. One of the men had circled around and stood in front of them.

"Games are over!" He lifted his revolver. "You're coming with us. The Colonel demands your presence and he really doesn't care much the shape you're in, as along as you can still open your mouths and tell he what he wants."

"No, we're not." Ashling yelled. "Game's over, buddy."

"No, it's not, little lady. Come with me. Now."

Liam drew her back behind him. A sound came from behind and they knew they were surrounded. Eddie looked around for his backup. They wouldn't know where they were.

Ashling shoved Liam aside. "No, we're not. Tell your friend behind us to drop his weapon."

The man behind them laughed. "Don't think so."

A sudden sound from above came to their ears. The two men looked up as did Liam and Eddie. Ashling grabbed at the two men with her and pulled. She knew what was coming but despaired of getting out of the way in time. An explosion sounded and threw them off their feet.

Eddie lay still for a moment and then stirred, lifting his head from the pavement. Ashling and Liam lay sprawled beside him. The two men at either end of the alley lay still. He shook his head. What had that been? Did he really want to know? It felt like someone had dropped a bomb on them.

He stood shakily and made his way to Liam and felt for a pulse. He was alive. Ashling was next. He could get a faint pulse from her but he had to really feel for it. A noise came from behind him and Ben and Caleb stood beside him.

"Are you all right, Caleb?" He eyed Caleb's left arm and the blood on it.

"I am. It hurts though. How are Liam and Ashling?" They could hear the sirens behind them, and then the sound of the stretcher wheels as the paramedics rushed in.

Ben went to check the two men at either end of the alley. He came back and shook his head. "They're dead, but it wasn't the explosion. Someone shot them."

Caleb spun around and then caught his balance as Eddie's hand came out to steady him. "Who?"

"I doubt we'll know. It wasn't one of us. I would think it was likely some of Ashling's friends from the streets. They protect their own."

Caleb nodded as he watched the paramedics working on his friends. Liam had been placed on a stretcher and was being wheeled away. They were still working on Ashling. She has been placed on a backboard and had neck support but the three watching saw that it was a lot more serious than they had thought. Sudden movement showed them intubating her and then starting CPR. She was rushed away.

Caleb's eyes slid shut in prayer. "Please, Lord, please. Don't let her die. Not when we're this close."

Ben's hand on his arm startled him. "We need to get you to the hospital too. You need that arm looked at."

Caleb started to refuse, then nodded. "You're right. You two can look after this scene. Find out what that explosion was though. I don't want a repeat of it any time soon."

* * * * * * * * * *

The Colonel stood at his office window, waiting. He had been promised those two would be here today and they weren't. Why? Had something happened?

He turned with a sense of foreboding. He looked around. He would need to leave soon, leave without the information that would secure his life and source for money.

* * * * * * * * * *

Leith and Regan ran for the Emergency Department. Laycee and Joshua were there waiting.

"Any word yet?" Leith hugged his sister, searching her face.

"No, no yet." Laycee clung to her brother. "I'm scared, Leith."

Leith's eyes met Joshua's over her head. "We'll pray, Laycee, we'll pray."

Joshua spoke, his voice raw with emotion. "That's what we can and will do. Caleb was shot today, too."

Regan spoke up. "Oh no, Joshua. How is he?"

Joshua shrugged. "He's still upright. He says it's nothing, Hannah says differently. She's back with him now, making sure he does what he's supposed to."

The four found seats and huddled together, heads bowed in prayer. They didn't look up as their pastor and others from their church family joined them.

Caleb looked over at Hannah. She stood just behind the doctor who was bandaging his arm. He had had to have stitches and knew that in a while, it was really going to hurt. But he wasn't done for the day, not for a while. Hannah's face was white and strained. Once the doctor had finished and left, he drew her to him and into a hug.

"Shhh. Hannah. Shhh. I'm fine. I'm coming home to you and the boys."

She clung to him. "I was so scared when Eddie called me. I thought it was worse."

Caleb felt his wife's tears and a few fell on her hair as he laid his head on her head. "God was watching."

He set her back and with hands on her arms, looked at her. "We need to find out how Liam and Ashling are. Have you heard anything?"

She shook her head. "I haven't but Eddie said they were still working on Ashling. Liam was going for X-Rays or a CT scan or something." Her hand came to her mouth. "What about Ashling's parents and brother? Are they here?"

Caleb's eyes slid closed. "I need to get out there. I need to talk to them." He staggered a bit as he slid down from the stretcher. He caught his wife's hand. "Come, let's go find them."

Caleb found Lachlan, Caitlin and Lorcan surrounded by the church family as were the other four. He stopped and spoke with each one of them. Joshua caught his brother in a hug and the two stood for a few minutes. No words needed to be spoken.

A sound behind them and they turned.

"I'm looking for Liam Bradley's family." The physician searched faces. The four went towards him and he drew them aside for some quiet conversation.

"Liam's pretty beat up, as you can imagine. Lots of bruises, scrapes but no broken bones. No internal injuries that we can see. He does have a concussion. He's still unconscious right now. We're going to be sending him up to a room shortly. If you want, two of you can go back with him for a few minutes." He watched as Laycee and Leith headed for the exam room where their brother lay.

Joshua spoke up. "Thank you, Doctor. That has put their minds at rest." He turned slightly to watch Ashling's family. "If you have news on Ashling Downie, her family's here."

The doctor drew a deep breath. "I'm not the physician that has her care. I'll see what I can find out for you. That's her family over there?"

Regan nodded. "Her parents and her brother."

He nodded and turned, hesitating. He knew the fight that was going on right now to save Ashling's life. Selfishly, he was glad he wasn't her physician.

About thirty minutes another physician entered the waiting room and headed for Ashling's family. Lachlan and Lorcan stood, grim looks on their faces, as they watched him approach them. They tried to read his face, but they couldn't.

He drew up a chair. "I'm Dr. Forrester. I've been working on your daughter." He hesitated and Caitlin's hand came to her mouth. He reached for her hand. "She's alive. We almost lost her a couple of times. We're taking her up to surgery right now. There's internal bleeding that we need to get under control." He looked up at her father and brother. "I need to tell you, she may not make it. We will do our best."

Caitlin gripped his hand. "She is in God's hands. If He wills she goes home today, that it what will happen. Please, our prayers are with you and the medical team."

He bowed his head and then looked at them. "Yes, that she is. I'll make sure you get regular updates."

Hours passed, and finally he returned. "She's in recovery. It was touch and go but your daughter is strong. I'll have someone come find you when we move her to an ICU room."

Caitlin's face was covered in her tears. She reached out to hug the doctor. "Thank you. God used you today."

Lachlan and then Lorcan reached to shake the physician's hand and thanked him. Lachlan then drew his wife and son into a hug and led them in prayer for his daughter's healing, for Liam and for Caleb, for wisdom of all concerned.

Chapter 20

Caleb stood at his desk and studied the paperwork in his hands. Warrants were issued and they were headed out shortly to serve them. It was not something he was looking forward to.

Ben knocked on his door and watched his friend. Caleb looked up and shook his head.

"I still don't understand. Do you?"

Ben shook his head. "No and I don't think I ever will."

Caleb and Ben and two officers entered Liam's office. His secretary looked up with a surprised look on her face.

"Where can we find Bud?" Caleb asked, regret in his voice.

"He is the lunch room, right down that hall." She stood and watched as the four made their way down the hall.

Caleb stood and watched Bud for a minute. "Bud."

As Bud turned and saw them, his face paled. "I guess this is it, isn't it?"

Caleb nodded. Ben read Bud his rights and then slipped the handcuffs on him.

"What I don't understand, Bud, is why?"

Bud shook his head. "Until you make another arrest, I'm not saying anything."

****

The Colonel stood watching out his window. He saw the cruisers that pulled up, saw Eddie climb out of one and stand looking at his house, then shake his head and move to follow the winding flagstone path to his front door. He heard his wife answer, heard her exclamation of surprise, a few quiet words spoken, and then a tap at the door.

It swung open and Eddie stood there, officers behind him. He studied the man in front of him.

"Dr. Young, you are under arrest for conspiracy to kidnap, murder, extortion, blackmail. I am sure we will find a few more charges to add to those." He nodded to one of the officers who slipped handcuffs on the once respected doctor. "I don't understand why."

"No, I don't suppose you would. I'm not saying anything without a lawyer." Still haughty, the physician was led from his home, his wife, in tears, left standing the hall.

Eddie stopped beside her, feeling sorry for a woman who had not always been kind, who quite often treated others in a way that belittled them. "He'll be in jail until his bail is made. Then he'll be going to trial. Do you have someone who can stay with you?"

Mrs. Young looked at him, and then she broke down. "I never knew. I'm sorry. I haven't treated people fairly or how I should have. Power and money, I guess, got to me. Now I have no one to turn to, not even my children."

"I'll speak with the pastor. He and his wife will come."

Eddie walked away from the house, shoulders slumped. It had been a bad day all around. His friend and boss had been shot and wounded, two other friends were in hospital, one that he wasn't sure was even going to make it, and now a prominent citizen had been arrested. But what bothered him the most was the betrayal directed at Liam. How Liam would deal with that, Eddie had no idea.

A voice spoke at his shoulder. "You found them, did you?"

"We did, Frankie, we did. Thank you for helping."

"How are Ashling and Liam?"

"Liam's got a concussion, lots of bruising.   Ashling."   Eddie's voice stopped. He swallowed hard. "She may not make it. She was in surgery a while ago."

Frankie's head dropped.   "I'm sorry. I didn't know they were going to drop what they did. I still haven't figured out what it was, but I will. Ashling has many friends down there."   He sighed and looked at the sky, then at Eddie. "I'm getting too old for this.   I think I need to come back in and drop the street name, go back to being a regular cop."

Eddie laid a hand on his shoulder. "Yes, Frankie, you do need to. What was your real name anyway?"

Frankie gave a short bark of laughter. "You know it well, Eddie, you know it well.   Tell Caleb I'll be in touch."

Leith and Laycee stood at their brother's bedside.   They knew he was still unconscious but they refused to leave until they knew he would be all right. The nurses had been in and out. Joshua and Regan were in the waiting room down the hall, spending the time in prayer.

Leith drew his sister close to him. She laid her head on her brother's shoulder.

"I am so glad he's alive." She said through her tears.

"I know. I know." Leith stopped, he couldn't continue.

"Have you heard yet how Ashling is?"

"Regan was going to see if she could find out."

"It will kill him slowly if she doesn't make it."

"I know. Come on, Laycee. We need to go and get some sleep. We don't have to leave the hospital. We can wait just down the hall."

Laycee reluctantly followed her brother from the room.

Lachlan and Caitlin stood at their daughter's bedside. Caitlin reached for Ashling's hand. The hiss and click of machines and monitors sounded through the room, IV dripped into her arm. Lorcan studied the equipment and then his sister. His eyes closed in prayer. Please, Lord, please heal her.

Dr. Forrester entered, chart in hand. "She's a fighter, your daughter is. I really didn't expect us to be standing here."

Lachlan spoke, the lump in his throat making it difficult. "She always had been, Doctor. She's been through stuff I can't imagine."

He finished his examination and then turned to them. "We were able to get the internal bleeding stopped. The spleen was removed, so we'll address that issue with her later. We'll gradually wean her off the pain medications we have her on and off all the equipment. I don't foresee any problems in doing that, barring any unexpected complications." His eyes turned to each one of them.

"But with the prayer that is going up for her, I doubt we'll have any of those." He turned and walked away.

Ashling's family were allowed to stay for a while longer and then sent down the hall to the waiting room. It would be a long few days for them. Friends had picked up duties at their store, so they had no worries. Lorcan would be in and out as he was on duty.

A week had passed. Liam had been discharged and had been working to sort out the problems at his work. He felt so betrayed by Bud, his foreman, someone who he thought had had his respect and liking. He still needed to confront him but that would come later.

He made his way back to the hospital. Ashling had been awake on and off for the last day or so and he wanted to spend some time with her. He stopped at her open door. A clean-cut man stood at her bedside, with short brown hair, dressed in a T-shirt, jeans and sneakers. Liam watched as he bent and dropped a kiss of Ashling's head and then turned.

The man walked towards Liam. Liam felt he knew him, but couldn't place him.

"She'll be fine, Eagle. Take care of her." A hand dropped on his shoulder and Frankie was gone.

Liam stared. That was Frankie? What had happened?

He drew up a chair to the bedside and sat. He reached for Ashling's hand, cradling it in his. They were really going to have to have a serious talk when she was well enough.

Ashling's fingers moved, and his eyes went to her face. She had turned to face him, a small smile showing. They needed no words right now. Those would come.

Chapter 21

Hannah stood on the Downie's deck and watched her husband and sons playing in the yard, Teagan bouncing around them. Caleb could finally put aside work for a day or two and spend time with his boys. Caitlin stopped beside her.

"It's good you could come today, Hannah. We needed to have you here. We can't thank you and Caleb enough."

Hannah shrugged. "It wasn't us, Caitlin, it was God."

Caitlin stopped her before she could continue. "God used you and Caleb." She turned to look over her deck at the people gathered. Their friends and family were there.

Ashling sat wrapped up in a warm blanket and snuggled down in a chair.

Liam stood behind her, hands on her shoulders. One day soon, they would talk. This was one lady he would not let get away.

Finally, as they had finished their meal, Lachlan turned to Caleb. "Tell us, Caleb. Tell us what you can."

Caleb looked around. This time, it had really hurt their community. It would take time to heal.

He shook his head. "I'm not sure if I even have all the facts. It's still an active investigation."

He continued. "Dr. Young had been involved blackmail and extortion for years, almost back to when he set up practice. I can't and won't give names. He had been putting money away in accounts under alternate names.

"The flash drive you found, Liam, that contained a list of those victims. Somehow, Bud found it and was doing some blackmailing of his own. We think when he did some work for Dr. Young, he did some snooping and helped himself to it. How he knew, he's not saying. He lost it when he was doing the work here. Not a real smart move to carry it on him all the time.

"Dr. Young thought Bud had lost it one day on the river bank where they were to meet and when you stooped to pick up something, he thought you had found it. He is the one who pushed you into the river."

Caleb paused and studied the sky. "The two men they hired. One was Mrs. Young's nephew, the other a nephew of Dr. Young's. He was the one that was murdered after the hit and run killed the Coles' boy. The other was from out of town. They may have had others involved and we think they did. The young Coles boy - his parents are adamant they don't know what he was up to. I can't prove otherwise. They have lost a son. We still haven't found out who shot the two men. No one will say, but Frankie thinks it was ones from the street, protecting Ember and her Eagle.

"Frankie has not been able to find out exactly what was dropped and there was only trace evidence. Our team thinks an explosive device but they don't have enough left to work with to determine exactly what and the quantities.

"We did find our leak once again in the department. It was a file clerk."

They sat in stunned silence at what Caleb had revealed.

Lachlan finally spoke. "I can't say that it amazes me the level people go to in the depravity. God will judge them." He stood, started to say something, then walked down the steps and away from them.

Ben and Eddie and their wives left not too long after. Life would go on and they would too. They needed time to heal.

Leith, Regan, Laycee, and Joshua all left next. Liam watched his family walk away and nodded. Yes, they would be fine. Each had found the mate God had for them and they would be stronger now then they had been.

Caleb and Hannah stood in front on the two.

Ashling looked up at Caleb. "Frankie - what will he do now?"

Caleb shook his head. "I'm not sure. He's resigned from the department. He hasn't said if he'll stay in town or not." Caleb's eyes met Liam's over Ashling's head and in Liam's, Caleb read the knowledge. Liam knew that Frankie had been in love with Ashling and now that she had made a choice that didn't include him, Frankie wasn't sure he could stay in the same town as she lived.

Hannah hugged Ashling and then the four Logans left, the two boys waving and asking if they could come back and play with Teagan.

Liam stood studying Ashling, then gathered her into his arms. She leaned her head back and studied him.

"You, my precious." Liam stopped. He dropped down into the chair she had been in. "I almost lost you. My heart couldn't take it if I had."

A hand came up and touched his face. "God knows, Liam, my eagle, my strong protector. Leave it with him." She turned to watch the sunset.

Epilogue

Liam caught up with Ashling as she walked the river bank three months later. The wind was chilly and clouds covered the sun. He wrapped an arm around her and stopped her.

She stood beside him, watching the water lapping at the river's edge.

"I never thought all those months ago that we would have such an adventure."

"Me, either." He turned her to face him. "Ashling, my precious, do you know what you do to my heart? When I thought I had lost you, I didn't know how I could ever go on?"

She dropped her eyes and laid her head on his chest. "Liam, don't. Don't go there. We've talked about it so many times, I just want to forget."

He hugged her tighter.

"So, my precious, this is where Laycee would be asking to go steady,

Leith to get engaged." He could feel Ashling starting to laugh. "I think we should just skip that step, the step of being engaged, and just get married. We can beat them at their own game."

She pushed away from him and stared. "What! No way, buster!. I have dreamed of years of being engaged and all that goes with it! You're not depriving me of that."

He stared in the sparkling blue eyes before him and laughed at her nonsense.

"Ashling, my precious, you are the one I love. Will you marry me?"

Ashling turned and Liam's heart fell. He had blown it big time.

Ashling giggled. Liam's eyebrows rose. She had giggled. He started to laugh.

"Ok, missy, turn around and look at me."

She did and nodded.

"Now, you just have to get past my Da and brother."

He smirked. "I already did. Your father gave his permission four months ago."

Her mouth dropped open. "Four months!"

He nodded. "He knew. Come on, my precious." He took her hand and led her towards the road and the way home.

"By the way, will you ever tell me why now I can hold your hand and before I couldn't?"

She slipped her hand from his and tucked it into his arm. "Because when my hand is tucked here, I am safe. I am close to you. Holding hands - it means you care. Like this, it means you are my protector. You have me close to your heart."

"I have been finding my way back to God and to peace. He has set my priorities straight once again." Liam looked down at her. "He has used you in a big way, my precious."

She drew him to a stop and then said, "The verse that has gone through my mind through all this has been the one about waiting on the Lord and renewing our strength, rising like an eagle. Frankie named you right. You really are an eagle."

He drew her close and then led her to the car, tucking her inside. He stopped, kissed her, and then said, "Eagles mate for life. You, my precious, are my mate for life."

Dear Readers

The third story in the Under His Wings trilogy is complete. It has been quite the ride, characters entering, demanding to be heard, fear, happiness. Through the series, I have attempted to show how much man's sin and depravity can affect those around them, but that with God, we can rise above what is around us. He provides us with wisdom, with strength, with honour, with trust, with truth. It has been my prayer throughout these books that you will turn and seek God in a richer, fuller way. Like Liam, we too can go through the motions of our Christian life, coasting along. This is not how God has intended that we walk with Him and in writing these books, particularly Liam's, I have been speaking to myself in a big way.

Characters changed their names and their occupations in my books. Plot lines changed. Dr. Young, the villain in The Eagle, was to be the villain in The

Sparrow and refused to cooperate with me.

My dear friend and sister in Christ, Faye Silvestro Kubassek, has once again taken on the task and proofread the story and made some suggestions to the story flow. Thank you, my dear friend. I really didn't mean to make you cry with this story. We have laughed and cried together so many times and sharing the occupation of medical secretaries has made our friendship so much deeper.

My parents have graduated to heaven. I miss them so much, particularly now when I have decisions to make about my books. I just want to sit down with them and hear their advice. They never steered me wrong. My father would shrug and tell me it was my decision but he always talked to me. My mother was the one who would be bold and blunt and tell me what she thought, and she was usually right. I miss their prayers, the joy they would have shared with me, my mother's smile of I knew you can do it, my father's you did a wonderful job. My first ever published novel, The Sparrow, was written on a challenge from my Mother. The Hawk and The Eagle flowed out of that book.

As I look to the future, characters in The Eagle are demanding their stories. I look forward to seeing what they will be up to. But rest assured, their lives will be centred on God.

God bless each one of you who have picked up one of my books and read it. I pray that you were blessed, challenged, and had a little bit of fun with trying to figure out who really did it before you got to the end. I enjoy a good mystery and have endeavoured to bring that in my stories.

My life verse is the one this book is based on: Isaiah 40:31: They that wait upon the Lord shall renew their strength, they shall mount up with wings as eagles, they shall run and not be weary, they shall walk and not faint.

Find your verse. God has one just for you.

With God's blessings and my thanks and love,

Ronna Bacon

www.ingramcontent.com/pod-product-compliance
Lightning Source LLC
Chambersburg PA
CBHW071556110726
47908CB00007B/2129